BOOKS BY G.R. MOUNTJOY

3 YEARS AFTER...
(A Military and Zombie Apocalypse Series)

3 YEARS AFTER...

{A MILITARY AND ZOMBIE APOCALYPSE SERIES}

G. R. MOUNTJOY

3 YEARS AFTER...
(A MILITARY AND ZOMBIE APOCALYPSE SERIES)
BY

G.R. MOUNTJOY

Seeker Element Publishing
First Paperback Edition June 2011

ISBN: 978-0615505794

Editing by: Monique Happy, Editorial Services
mohappy@att.net

Cover Design by Danzig Designs

For more information about the book or author visit Facebook under Gary R. Mountjoy or http://3yearsafterbook.blogspot.com/.

3 YEARS AFTER

A Military and Zombie Apocalypse Series

SEEKER ● ELEMENT ● PUBLISHING

CHAPTER 1
WALTER REED AND THE CHOICE

CPT Ryder Mountjoy stood and rubbed his sore shoulder. Days were turning into weeks at Walter Reed Army Hospital. Since his return from Afghanistan to recuperate and recover from his wounds, he had been forced to submit to the torture of the physical therapists. Therapy was one thing, but the extreme amounts of pain while trying to regain strength, movement, and the use of his left arm were becoming pure torture. In the back of his mind, he thought that they actually enjoyed dealing out the extreme amounts of punishment that he was being subjected to. At least if things went well he would be back to Fort Bragg and back in the swing of things in no time. The hospital was an amazing place. Surgeries, prosthetics, and medical procedures were saving soldiers, sailors, marines and airman like no other time in history, and for this he was thankful.

Breakfast came: Eggs, bacon, coffee, fresh fruit, and even a bagel with cream cheese. This was much better than the shit he was used to living on while on deployment. From Southeast Asia, Iraq, Afghanistan, and many shitholes in the Philippines, Africa and South America, life was good when food was good. At 0830 when the orderly usually showed up to take him to the rack as Mountjoy had begun to refer to it, a man in a black suit showed up instead.

Mountjoy looked at the man and instantly thought of Tommy Lee Jones in the movie Men in Black. The man came in, told him that his name was Mr. Black (which Mountjoy thought was ironic), and that he needed Captain Mountjoy to come with him for a briefing. This wasn't unusual, but it had been 12 days since he had briefed a couple of Generals, Admirals, and a few Company men on the events that led to his near death experience in the mountains of Pakistan.

Without hesitation he pulled on his boots, much better than the damn slippers and robe that he had been wearing at first, and told Mr. Black to lead the way. Mr. Black laughed, explained that this wasn't going to take very long, and advised Captain Mountjoy to go ahead and get the rest of his uniform on. Grabbing the top to his ACU uniform, green beret, and wallet, he followed Mr. Black down the hallway and into the elevator. The elevator doors hissed open and they entered into the confined space of the elevator. Until this point, things had appeared to be normal, until Mr. Black pulled out a key and put it into the slot. CPT Mountjoy laughed a little and made the comment, "5th floor, Ladies Underwear, hmmm, Mr. Taylor?", and then laughed it off. Mr. Black's expression didn't change. The elevator went down and the doors opened.

As soon as he stepped out, Mountjoy realized that this was one of the underground passageways that most government buildings had, and that Mr. Black might or might not be taking him to an official debriefing. While working as an operative, Mountjoy had been privy to see some of the things inside of our government that are said not to exist, but hell, he was a shooter, so it really was not that much of a concern to him.

Mr. Black led the way down the hallway to a closed door, got his keys back out, opened the door and told CPT Mountjoy to follow him. Inside the door was a normal briefing room, and there were three other men sitting at tables waiting for whoever was going to lead this briefing. CPT Mountjoy took a seat at the fourth chair that was unoccupied and said hello to the other people in the room. It looked as if one was Army, the next one either a sailor or Marine, and the third was in his robe and slippers, unshaven and needing a haircut. Mr. Black picked up a phone on the wall, said something into the receiver and told the 4 that the briefing would start in a few minutes. At this time Mr. Black left the room and closed the door behind him.

Now this is when most soldiers start to talk, ask each other what and why they are here, their ranks, where they are from and other military chitchat. Mountjoy could tell that this was a group of unique personnel since none of this was happening. Most soldiers start to shoot the breeze as soon as they can, but not this group. All proved in the next sixteen minutes of waiting to be cool and collected, and to have no idea what or who they were waiting for.

The door at the other side of the room opened, and in stepped a 4 star General that everyone had seen or heard of, General David Smith, Chairman of the Joint Chiefs of Staff, an older man that appeared to be in his early 60's wearing a suit and a tie. Behind the suit came a doctor wearing a lab coat and scrubs. This was by no means an interesting development to any of those seated in this room, but Mountjoy thought that it sure was strange to have a cloak and dagger type briefing with a few strangers, and the Chairman.

CPT Mountjoy got to his feet and said, "Group, Attn'Hut!" All four immediately snapped to attention, which was followed by General Smith saying "As you were." The General was wearing Dress Blues, the new dress uniform for the Army, and asked everyone to have a seat

The General cleared his throat and began. "Gentlemen, you have been brought here today by events that none of you ever thought would happen. All four of you are highly trained, have individual skills, and training that our country needs today and in the future. I hope that in the next few hours this briefing will shed some light on why you are here, the mission you are going to be asked to participate in, and the need that our nation has to make this work. Mountjoy thought, 'Mission, hell, I'm still on the mend, what damn mission?' The Gen then told them that the man in the suit was from the NSA, and that he could be referred to as Mr. Frank, and the physician was from NASA and was named Dr. Williams. Mr. Frank and Dr. Williams would be presenting the mission to the men, and the Gen was there to prove to them that what they would learn in the next few hours wasn't a hoax, and that all of what was being presented was true.

Mr. Frank started his part of the briefing by asking if anyone thought time travel was possible. All four men laughed, and there was even a wise crack by the guy in the robe referring to Star Gates and some other nonsense.

Mr. Frank continued. "Gentlemen, the United States has stumbled upon some technology, and we think that we can actually send people through time. This could be monumental, but we hardly know anything about it. There are concerns about messing with the flow of time and about using this technology for good vs. evil. The President himself thinks that if this works, then we could possibly go back a few days, hours or minutes and change things that go catastrophically wrong into nothing more than a bad memory for the people that we would send back. This technology could save the world, keep wars from escalating, stop terrorist attacks, even keep the stock market in check. Of course you are only here because of your security clearances, and if any one of you feel that this is wrong, or too far fetched, or hell, even not worth the amount of danger pay that you would receive to be part of this experience, let us know, and you will be released."

At this point Gen. Smith stepped in and said "The people in this room have just about as high of a security clearance as you can get without being the Chairman of the Joint Chiefs, The President,

The Director of the CIA, or anyone else in the Pentagon for that matter. The fact that you are here in Walter Reed is just icing on the cake. The president gave the order last week to select a team, and to be honest gentlemen, you are about as good as they come. To start with, no one here has any secrets that can't be shared in this room. I will start with telling each of you about each other, then we will take a break, you can shake each other down, have lunch, talk among yourselves, and then let us know if you think you can handle doing something bigger than you've ever dreamed of for yourselves and your nation. Gentlemen, let me be clear, this is a dangerous mission, and your sacrifice will not go unnoticed or unrewarded. Let's get started with some introductions."

"Mathew B. McShea, MSG United States Army (RET), you are here at Walter Reed for an evaluation for sleep apnea. You are currently a member of the NSA working EOD, and you have done wet ops in Europe, North Africa, and the Persian Gulf. Member before retirement of 7th Special Forces Group, you actually completed B.U.D.S, Halo, and when on active duty were an 18 series demolition specialist. Damn son, sleep apnea?"

"Sir, my dog can't stand the snoring, ha-ha."

"Well that is just dandy, son, that is an impressive résumé that you have." The General moved on to the next man.

"CW4 Scott Riloh, US Army. Former member of Force Recon, now an Army Blackhawk pilot with 17 years of active duty. Been through Army Ranger School, Force Recon Training, Army Jump and Halo courses, Anti-Terrorist and sniper training. Why the hell did we let you go to Flight school, you are a damn killer, son. I guess that we just sometimes let people do what they want. Good thing I wasn't your CO, you would have been in Force Recon till this day, young man."

Riloh said to the General, "Sir, just trying to get more out of life, that's all."

"And you are here for a hearing test, a simple coincidence," the General remarked.

"Former Petty Officer/LT Kris McGilvra, now a member of the Secret Service. You are here because of a gunshot wound to the thigh, going home in a week. Are you good to go? Or is it just too nice here for you to have a few days off?"

"Sir, my Boss told me to milk it, said I needed a vacation," McGilvra responded.

"You took a bullet for the Secretary of Defense after an assassination attempt last month, great going young man, your country needs heroes. Let's see, for starters you were a SEAL, have completed training in all environments, have a background in communications, and are a shooter. You are a great fit also."

The General then turned to the last man at the table. "CPT Ryder Mountjoy, West Point class of 2004, Ranger School, Special Forces Selection, and now a team leader in DELTA. You have competed HALO, Jump School, and are a shooter also. You are the team leader; these men will all work for you if you guys decide to take this mission. Any questions CPT Mountjoy?"

"None, Sir!"

"CPT Mountjoy, that arm wound good to go?"

"Yes Sir, it is," CPT Mountjoy responded promptly.

General Smith concluded the basic briefing. "OK men, Mr. Black will take you to another room, lunch will be served, you can have some time to talk among yourselves, and we will reconvene in one hour to make some decisions. I know that this isn't easy, but we have a short time span to complete our selection, and the four of you almost fit the mission profile to a T. You were all selected because you have no children, and at the moment have no wives. Two of you are divorced, and the other two look to be married to your jobs. That is it, gentlemen, have a good lunch and see you back here in an hour."

At that point they were escorted into the next room where lunch was waiting, and Mr. Black left them to eat. Riloh sat down and started in by saying, "Well guys, what the hell do you think, and are we on Funniest Home Videos?"

All of them sat and ate, a little small talk, and almost as one they all started to laugh. McGilvra said, "Did he say something about a lot more danger pay? Shit, I would do it for almost free if they really have this operational." All four men looked at one another, and as one they decided it was a go.

They finished eating, called Mr. Black in and asked him to inform the General that they were all good to go, and that they didn't need an hour to figure it out. Mr. Black stepped out the side door without saying anything, then returned about two minutes later. "Gentlemen, follow me." It always made Mountjoy laugh to himself when these suits kept their sunglasses on, now it seems that he would be working with two of them. Oh well, he was from an elite unit, and other people loathed what they wore, and how they acted also.

When they went back to the briefing room, no one was inside; Mr. Black told them to have a seat, and the General would be with them shortly. All four took their seats, and did what experienced operators do, they examined the room in a nonchalant way and waited patiently. After about fifteen minutes the door opened, and in walked the Chairman of the Joint Chiefs again, followed by the Secretary of Defense, and the President of the United States. All four snapped to attention and stood like sentinels.

President Striker said, " As you were gentlemen," and the four sat back down as one. President Striker came forward, shook each man's hand, told them that he appreciated them taking time out of their busy schedules, and that this was as important a mission as there ever would be. He stepped back up to the General, shook his hand, said a few hushed words, then looked back at the group and said, "Gotta get the old cholesterol checked today. Once again, thank you gentlemen, I can't begin to express how important this is." After another round of salutes, he and the Sec-Def left through the door that they had entered.

The General cleared his throat and began again. "With that, men, we are a go, we will ship out this afternoon. Mr. Black and his men are gathering your belongings. From this moment until mission completion you are all under my direct supervision, no calls in or out, and I will see you topside at the landing pad in 30 mikes."

All four snapped to attention, and with that the General left them with an agent.

"OK guys, my name is Mr. Orange, you will come with me. We are going to get you dressed and on the way to meet the General."

Mr. Orange led them down the hall and into a locker room. This room had racks of clothing, everything from simple to all forms of camouflage to dress cloths. Mr. Orange said, "Go ahead and get something to wear, not to dressy, not too casual, and not anything that makes you stand out. We will be leaving in 10 mikes, go ahead and take the time to pick something out, and for God's sakes, don't come out looking like G.I. Joe. The President is in the building, and if we run into the press corps and you look like mercenaries we will have a metric shit ton of media asking him questions."

All four got dressed, boots, jeans or khaki cargo pants, shirts, from polos to button ups, and all the ins and outs. McShea made the comment "Man, this place is like a candy store for you to pick from, your everyday merc to Anti –Trust Lawyer could find something to wear in here." Everybody chuckled.

After ten minutes, Mr. Orange returned and led them to an elevator, pulled out a key, and pushed the button for roof access. Mountjoy knew the layout well; in his life with DELTA they had practiced in a plethora of environments, and even done some missions in downtown D.C. to practice anti-terrorist operations. Most buildings with a heli-pad had a key access point for the roof.

It seemed that no one in the group was too concerned about what was going on. It was just another mission, another way to eke out an existence working for the government, and another way to make their nation proud.

On the roof was the General waiting for them. He had a Major with him who was probably their aide, and of course there was a Blackhawk. The four-man team along with Mr. Black and Mr. Orange, the General and his aide boarded up and put on their Dave Clark headphones. The General gave the crew chief a thumbs up, and they were airborne within a minute. The General's voice came over the mike. "Gentlemen, the flight is a short one, we are headed to Andrews to meet up with the plane, then we will be en route to a small National Guard post with an underground facility in rural Indiana. We should be there in about 3 hours, so when we get on the plane we will have another briefing and go over some details."

The flight to Andrews took about thirty minutes; with all the corridors and flight patterns that even the Army had to take around D.C. since 9/11 it wasn't a direct flight. They touched down near a Gulfstream G-5 and were greeted by two Navy Pilots. It would be a wise bet that this was the Chairman's personal flight crew, since they saluted and went straight to the cockpit; no dog and pony show for the highest ranking man in the military. Upon boarding the plane, all four saw their personal effects in the storage locker that remained open, the doctor that had never said a word at Walter Reed, and a table that could comfortably seat all six men. Mr. Black and Mr. Orange took the seats closest to the cockpit, and the General told them they could have the next few hours to take a break. Mountjoy wondered if they were his personal bodyguards or some sort of team assigned by the NSA, FBI, CIA, or some other part of the government. Not that it mattered, they worked for him and did whatever the General told them to do.

At this point all four of the team members took a seat; the

General sat down, along with the doctor who had yet to be named. The flight would take about 2 hours and 25 minutes from takeoff to landing, and they were all advised by the Captain of the plane that they should buckle up and they would be taking off soon. The General told everyone that there was a refrigerator in the back if they needed anything to drink or eat, and that they would start the rest of the briefing once they were airborne. Mr. Black came to the table, asked if anyone needed anything, and then took his seat. The plane started rolling and the passengers all put their seats into the forward position for takeoff. Under five minutes later they were in the air, and all had moved back into the position facing the table.

General Smith smiled grimly at them all and began. "Gentlemen, you have all been selected and have accepted this assignment. You are now part of a Unit that is known as the 'Seeker Element.' At this point in time, I would like for you all to select a code name. Some of you have been in Units that use these names on a daily basis, a call sign if you will. We are having you do this for contingency plans. You will all have a call sign that is attached to your unit designation. If something were to go catastrophically wrong and you ended up in some sort of predicament, if the mission or experiment goes wrong, you can go to any government facility, embassy, or liaison and have them use your unit designation and call sign and you will be taken in a serious manner. Some of you have done this before, some haven't. But be assured, it is part of close unit interaction and from this point onward you should try getting used to using these names. Now I know you have all seen movies with such call signs, and have nicknames that people close to you use. I'm going to give you a minute to figure out what you want your call sign to be, and then once you pick one it is yours. I know this may sound like a moot point, but these call signs will go into the database at Langley and other redundant systems in the United States and worldwide, and God help us, may be your link to civilization if something doesn't quite work out right for the team."

"Let me go first," said General Smith. At this all four gave looks, raised eyebrows or small smiles.

"Oh yeah, I forgot to tell you, I also am taking a call sign since this little unit is my dream child. I will now be called "Honcho," no more of this General crap. I was in the jungles of Vietnam, Grenada, Panama, Desert Storm 1 and 2, and have a little time here and there when I was with SOCOM."

"Captain Mountjoy, or should I say Col. Mountjoy. Which reminds me, you all have been promoted and will be using your new ranks and pay grades for operational situations. And by the way also, the promotions are permanent, and the President has signed off on them. This unit is a career unit, you will not leave, the only way out is retirement, and you can stay active as long as you can stay fit. I hope that with that and the amount of danger pay, jump pay, flight pay, dive pay, sea pay, and Professional pay that you will now receive will be a little incentive for what you will be doing for our Nation."

All four were smiling like school children that had just been given A's for the year.

The General continued, "There will be some other surprises when we get to Atterbury, but until then, let's get to work on the call signs and go from there.

"Col. Mountjoy, what call sign would you like to choose?"

"Sir, I will go with Achilles, simple and to the point. Besides I never liked being called my other name in DELTA, I just thought that choosing this as a call sign was better than Westy." With this there was some laughter from the group, everyone picking up from the Unit call sign that the NCOs' had obviously bestowed on the officer and West Point Grad.

"Maj. McGilvra, your turn, what do you choose?"

"I will go with Meat, some of my buddies used to call me that, old joke, but it's a name that I can live with and have no issues with anyone calling me that. Nothing to tell really, just one of my buddies called me that and it stuck."

"CW5 Riloh, what do you choose to call yourself?"

"Well, Honcho," Riloh began, the first time anyone had referred to the General as anything but Sir or General, it was common for Aviators to be lax, "I will go with Hollywood. Love the name from watching that movie Top Gun, too bad the pilot in that movie never really did anything important, and in Task Force we only use Company and number designation."

"CSM McShea, anything that you have that will make us laugh?"

"Well, I just love a name that I used to play a video game with in my spare time. In case no one knows it, I'm a bit of a computer geek, and that may be another reason that the Honcho chose me. I will go with Moonclavian, or Moon for short. It was the name I used for a character in World of Warcraft. No biggie, just one that I am also used to answering to.

Honcho nodded and began the more serious part of the briefing. "Now that all of you have your new ranks, new call signs, and know a little about each other, we have the operational leadership to go over. Of course I am in charge, well, the President is in charge. We will call him Eagle, but of course never to his face. I am second in command. Then we have Achilles, Meat, Hollywood, and Moonclavian. Now that everything is set, you will now meet the Doc. Since he is an M.D., we decided that the call sign fit him. He is a civilian and will be under my command also. There is a team that is at Atterbury; they all work for us also. Now the Doc will give his part of the briefing. We decided to hold off until everyone stepped up and took the assignment to complete the briefing."

Doc stepped forward and looked each of them in the eyes. "Gentlemen, you are now part of what has been code named 'Project Dark-star.' Our mission is to send you guys 3 years into the future, and then bring you back. We have done this with a few monkeys and with lab rats. There are no side effects, and they have all made it back. What we lack right now is the human team to go forward, run some tests, return and then do follow up missions as assigned by the President. If everything works out, in 48 hours we will be mission complete, and you will be back in D.C. awaiting your next mission. We can change the world, stop dictators, find cures for illnesses, avoid financial ruin, stop terrorists, and even stop wars before they happen. We have decided upon the 3 year time frame since everything that was done in that timeframe so far has worked out, animals have returned unscathed and things in the future appear to happen in time with the current. As I have said, they have returned, so we seem to think that the theories of time travel and that time is in constant motion appear to all have been true. Some of the top scientists from places such as Area 51, NASA, and others have come together to make this mission real instead of just fantasy."

With this, Moon spoke up and asked a question. "Honcho, are you telling us that Area 51 really does have something going on? That it isn't just a range where weapons are tested?"

Honcho laughed. "Gentlemen, there are many things that you will learn in the next few weeks and months. I hope you are in for a long interesting trip, because when I became the Chairman, I was introduced to things that were beyond belief. There are only a few people in the government that have higher security clearances than those seated at this table." Honcho continued. "Also, we will never travel into the past, the only time that will happen is when we return you to the present. We have a window of 72 hours backwards that we can travel to, tests beyond that have been sanctioned off limits, no messing with the past. We are going to try forward first, then backward in time. The two jumps that you will make are designed and have worked so far. This should be interesting."

For the rest of the flight the group just talked, told a few stories about why they were in Walter Reed, places that they had been, hell holes that they had fought in, and a little about each other. The Captain of the Gulfstream announced that they were on their final descent; everyone turned their chairs forward and prepared for landing.

CHAPTER 2
CAMP ATTERBURY

Upon landing, they were met on the small airfield by two black Chevrolet Suburbans. Of course, it was always Suburbans or Land Rovers depending on which government agency was controlling an operation. Honcho gave the pilots some instructions, telling them to go ahead and head over to Indianapolis International Airport and wait for the call to return to pick them up. Since this operation was secret, if daylight struck and members of the National Guard saw a Gulfstream G-5 sitting on the runway, they might realize that something or someone was around. That was another reason that they never took off or landed during the daytime while visiting Atterbury. The team disembarked and were introduced to the two remaining members of the Chairman's Men in Black. They were to be called Mr. Brown and Mr. White. This almost made Moon and the other laugh. They had all seen the Tarantino movie from the 1990's, Reservoir Dogs, and in the movie the main characters were all designated by colors. Moon looked at Honcho and asked him where Mr. Pink was at; Honcho laughed and replied that at least someone else finally got the joke.

Seeker Element was then whisked away via the SUV's and down a few roads and turns. They came upon a dead end, Mr. Brown hit a button and the roadblock dropped. They then went right past it and into what looked like a dense forest. For a moment, the members of the team all thought that they were going to crash, but they continued through the mirage unscathed.

Honcho turned to them and made the comment, "Freaked me out the first time I went through one of those things, the Nerds call them mirages, but it's actually an active camouflage that we are working on. Can't put it into uniforms yet, but works great to make something like a wall or forest appear as a dead end." They then entered drove straight into the side of a hill, which turned out to be the same type of mirage. It was actually a large tunnel.

The SUV's came to stop inside what could only be described as a large underground hanger. There were all sorts of things going on, no less than fifty people moving to and fro around, welding and all of it looking like something out of a space movie. The team got out and Honcho told them to follow Messrs. White and Brown to the living quarters. They moved along the wall to a door, the outside of which was marked with the standard military markings as Living and Berthing Quarters.

"Looks like there were people from the Army and the Navy that made the signs here," remarked Moon.

They passed through the door and entered into a hallway, where Mr. Brown told them that they were to have the room marked 113B. It was straight down and on the right side of the hallway. Then he pointed to a sign that said Briefing Room. "Drop your stuff and come back this way. We will meet Honcho, the Doc, and Number 1 here in about 10 mikes." Mr. Brown then turned and strode away.

They went down the hall about thirty feet and found the door. Inside was a standard bay style barracks room for four people to co-habitat in. There were two showers, two commodes, and two sinks through a door adjoining the room. Each man chose a bunk, placed their gear on top of it, and took a moment to go to the bathroom or wash up. Then the group went back down the hall to the briefing room. They entered and found that Honcho, the Doc, and a stranger they could only guess was 'Number 1' were already sitting at a table waiting on them.

"Gentlemen," Honcho said, "Feel free to grab some coffee from the Silver Bullet (Military Lingo for Coffee Maker) in the corner." Moon and Hollywood each grabbed a cup of java, Meat took a pass and sat down, and Achilles grabbed a plastic cup and a bottle of water.

"Hey Achilles, you got a pinch on you?" Meat was asking for some of the Copenhagen snuff that Achilles had on him. At that, Honcho said "Shit, that's what I'm talking about," and pulled out an unlit cigar and started chewing on it. "Sorry men, I just was waiting for someone to ask for a smoke or something before I got out a stogie. Don't worry, I won't light up inside, just love to chew on them these days."

"OK team," Honcho said, "This is Number 1. He is a scientist from the unnamed facility in the Desert that you all call Area 51. He's in charge with the help of the Doc. You can call him Number 1, he works for me, and he has already read your backgrounds and bios. He has had access to your fiche and restricted fiche for the past 2 weeks and helped in the selection process."

Number 1 leaned forward and smiled genially at the group. "Gentlemen, it's nice to meet you. We will have some food brought in a few minutes, and then you can have some downtime. We will get busy tomorrow morning. I have two jumps planned for you. Initially, you will go forward in time 6 hours. We will be here waiting for your return, then we will do some tests. Later in the afternoon you will go forward 3 days. Tests will be run, and then you will be sent back in time to prior to your first jump. This will reset everything, contrary to popular belief; you cannot exist so far as we can tell in both timelines. If we send you forward, all of you goes forward. No part of you stays in the past. If you go back, you are *you* when you get there. The "present " you ceases to exist. All of the mumbo jumbo in Back to the Future about running into yourself is nonsense as far as we can tell. We have conducted quite a few jumps with the chimps and rats, we think that this will confirm everything."

Honcho spoke up at this time, "Thank you Number 1. Ah, dinner is here," as Mr. Black came in with pizza. He placed it on the table, looked around and announced, "Gentlemen, this isn't the run of the mill pizza that you have had before. This is from a place about 45 minutes away, it's the General's favorite. The restaurant is called the New Bethel Ordinary in Wanamaker. It's a little stop light of a town outside of Indianapolis. We had some state troopers drive it here to keep it warm. Told them that there were a few big shots that wanted pizza, being a spook has its privileges." He laughed and left the room.

Honcho and the rest of the four team members remained; everyone else left. This was almost like it was preplanned, a leader and his men having a quiet dinner before the storm, at least that is what Achilles thought anyway.

"Men," Honcho said. "This mission is going to be a great thing for our country. I want you to put together a list of supplies that you will carry on yourselves. I guess you can call it a packing list. Get uniformed, weapons, ammo, commo, rations, explosives, and whatever you need. I know that everyone thinks that this is going to be a walk in the park, send you forward, meet you, test you, and then you end up right back here, but just like any other dangerous mission, you need to have your shit together and be locked and loaded." With that there was the unison of Ho-aah's from the team (a common phrase for 'good to go,' or for just saying something to avoid saying 'yes' and 'no' to someone in charge.) Honcho continued, "Take a little while to finish eating, then go into the main hanger. Mr. Black will be waiting to take you to supply, then to the Armory. I want you men to be ready to rock and roll before you hit the sack. Also, you now have full permission to carry a weapon on or off duty. You only report to myself and the President, so I have decided that you can pack your heat at all times. Everyone got it?" There was a chorus of 'yes sirs.'

After dinner the team went on the walk to the hanger. On cue, out strolled Mr. Black from a side door. 'This place is big,' was all that Meat thought to himself. Mr. Black led them to the adjacent side of the hanger and into a door that said "Armory and Supply," simple enough phrasing, but with armory you could bet that supply was for shooting and not for scientists. Inside they came to what looked to be a room the size of a single aircraft hanger. There was a desk and a man reading a book, who upon seeing them jumped to his feet.

"Hello Gentlemen, my name is Tinker, everyone here has call signs, that one is mine. Honcho told me you are the travelers, and that you were to get whatever you need.

"Hi Tinker, I am Achilles, team lead and these are the rest of the fine men on the team. OK guys, let's start with basic needs. We all should wear standard ACU's, boots, fleece, skivvies, t-shirts, socks (six pairs), and two of everything else."

At this point Hollywood spoke up. "Do you have any of the Aviation ACU's? Boss, they might be handy, they are flame retardant like flight suits, could be useful just in case."

Achilles nodded his head. "Great idea, and we need belts, stocking caps, general type stuff in case we need to spend a couple of nights on the run in the future."

Next came the equipment. All four got throat mics and ear pieces, radios, a longer range Sincgars radio, combat vest, Kevlar, Spec- Ops type 1 combat helmets (more like bicycles or mountain climbing types), Oakley eyewear with photo-chromatic lens, night vision reticules, GPS units, knee and elbow pads, fifty feet of rope each, rappel harness, and all the ins and outs.

"Say, Tinker, who is the armorer and where is he located?"

asked Achilles, and Tinker smiled. "That would be me, Sir, and I was about to get to that next. What type of weapons are needed?"

Achilles thought for a moment before he answered. "Well, since we are all shooters, what do you guys think?"

Moon started in and said that they should carry Heckler and Koch .45 ACPs in combat holsters, and probably back up micro compact on boot holsters. "Just like some of you guys have used, we know that that model can survive salt water, sand, and cold weather, may be the best choice we have for side-arms. Also, Achilles, we should probably carry 250 rounds each, enough for close combat and such."

"Great idea," said Achilles, "that's what I'm talking about. OK, onto long arms."

"We should all carry suppressors for each," came Meat's voice. "Can you make that happen, Tinker?"

Tinker nodded. "For the standard .45 H&K's that is no problem, the backup hold outs cannot be fit in a hurry. I can make that happen and have them ready before you return to D.C. though. That way you can have suppressors that work on both pistols."

Achilles went on with his list. "Long arms, we should all carry either M-4's with suppressors with laser designators, or MP-5's for that matter. I actually think that M-4's would work, and they can be suppressed also, we had them in DELTA. Tinker, do you have four?"

At that point Hollywood spoke up. "We need an M-24, spotter scope, and we need to cross-load it, break it down, and also 500 rounds of ammo."

"Great thinking. Tinker, do you have one pound blocks of C-4, det. cord, and blasting caps?" said Moon.

"Oh, yeah," Tinker responded, "already ahead of you on that one."

Achilles stood with the team chatting, while Tinker took about fifteen minutes getting the firearms, ammo, explosives and the rest of the gear together and making out a hand receipt. That made the members laugh, they still were slaves to signing for stuff from supply. They took the time to cross-load, check their gear, load it into the Blackhawk backpacks that they had requested, got ins and outs such as survival knives, bench made switch-blade type knives, camel-back water systems, and matches, compasses, water resistant matches, boonie caps, Oakley gloves, and water purification tablets. At that point Tinker came back and had four cases with him.

"Gentlemen, these are what we are referring to as Pad's, they are kind of like the Apple IPAD, but they are a government super mini-computer. Inside you will find roll up solar chargers, and they can even operate like satellite phones with video. There is also a Blue Tooth headset that will work with them. You can keep them in the pouch on top of your backpacks. You'll have a three mile range in bad situations such as urban environments, and a twenty mile range in the open for voice communication. Is there a computer hacker or geek here in the squad?" asked Tinker. With that Moon stepped forward; he was given a tool kit, can of air, and enough little odds and ends to fix Pads if needed.

Tinker continued proudly. "These are basically better than anything that is in the Government inventory. There are security hacks, and even ways to control things such as drones and other stuff. Honcho has the only other one that I have issued. Familiarize yourselves with them and have a blast."

With that it was nearing 2200 hours, so the team made their way back to Room 113B and got settled in for the night. After only a few minutes, Honcho came in with his duffle bag, and proceeded to get settled into one of the top bunks that wasn't taken. "Hello Achilles," he said, "thought I would bunk with my team before the mission." Achilles got up, shook his hand, told him the rest of the guys were showering, cleaning up, shaving and doing the other personal hygiene things that needed to be accomplished, and that Honcho was more than welcome to come in with the men.

"Achilles, it is good that we have a moment. I know that today has been a whirlwind, things have gone from being in a hospital to being back on duty. In your assessment is the team ready to go, and are your wounds good to go?"

"To be honest," Achilles replied, "I am wired tight and so are the rest of the guys. We are doing something that hasn't been done before, and we are ready to go for a combat mission. When you came in, I thought you were going to get on my ass about all the gear we took, and the fact that we look like modern day John Rambo's to be honest Sir!"

"No concerns about that, son, we knew that you guys would take certain items, and to be honest, you need to and have done a great job selecting equipment. Tinker is coming with a few more items that he told me you guys had to take with you, shouldn't add but a few more pounds to your tactical gear, and to be honest he had some great ideas he came to me with right after you walked out."

As if on cue, Tinker came into the squad bay with a pack slung over his shoulder which he quickly unloaded. He had four pistol grip 22-inch shotguns, complete with backpack quick draw over the shoulder holsters. He also had two M-203 grenade launchers for under two of the M-4 carbines that they had selected. With this there were 48 "203" rounds, flichete and High Explosive, and also 24 shotgun rounds per person. "I know that this will add to the weight, Achilles, but you should all be under ninety pounds, a load that everyone here can handle. I hope that is OK, just last minute details that I thought you guys might like to have." With that, Achilles thanked Tinker, and said "Great thinking Tink, we do appreciate it." Achilles wasn't sure if he liked being called Tink, but he didn't say anything so Achilles assumed the nickname was copacetic.

After that, the other members of the team came in to the

squad bay. They had finished their personal hygiene and came back from the latrine, or as Hollywood still referred to it from his days in the Marines, the "Head." They all greeted Honcho, then Achilles said he was going to get cleaned up, and let the team know that they were under relaxed grooming standards: beards, moustaches, goatee's and long hair could be worn. Honcho got a kick out of this, since all the men had just clean shaven themselves.

It was approaching 2300 hours, everyone was playing with their PADS. Moon was getting a kick out of it, no email was to be sent, but they all knew the rules and could be trusted. Honcho said that lights out was 2300, first call would be 0630, and they would have breakfast, and then have around 2 hours to practice some squad type movements and other things before a briefing at 1000 hrs. He finished with "If anyone wants to use the gym, or run, there's one down the hallway that could accommodate you; feel free to use it."

Night turned into morning after what was a good night's worth of sleep for everyone. At 0630 Honcho was up, and everyone rose and did their usual morning stretching and got dressed. At this point Achilles thought of a problem. He decided that once everyone got finished cleaning up and getting dressed that they should talk about it as a cohesive unit.

"Honcho, Sir, I have a question that I think we should weigh over before going operational. We are short one thing in this group, and that's a medic. Specifically, a Warrant or Commissioned 18D series that can do field surgery, and know what to do if we get hit or something."

Honcho looked at him in admiration. "Holy shit, I knew we selected you because you are one smart SOB Achilles, I hadn't thought of that, and no one else in the think tank here even brought that up. We are supposed to go operational today, and that is going to be a problem. Anyone have any suggestions?"

With that it was Moon who had a great idea. "Sir, I know

that we aren't in D.C., Fort Bragg or anywhere else, but I have a friend from my days in 7th Group. He actually served 14 years, then decided to get out. He is in a Long Range Surveillance Detachment in the Indiana National Guard, and 18D, CW2. He is a team leader. We play World of Warcraft together, and still talk almost weekly when we have a chance. He is the same age as me, we went to Basic and the 82nd together, then assessed for SF, and were on the same team for 4 years. He is an ICE agent with U.S Customs and Border Patrol. Hell, Sir, he isn't more than a half hour from here, his post is in downtown Indianapolis."

"God Damn Sergeant Major, you are one good retired NCO if I have ever met one, come with me, let's get to the Op Center and see what we can dig up on your old buddy. Achilles, with us, Hollywood and Meat, we will meet you at 0730 at the mess, it's down this hallway a quarter mile, you can't miss the smell of the great food that they make here." With that, Honcho, Achilles, and Moon went to the Op Center.

They didn't even know what half this facility was, in all fairness they had just seen about a quarter of what was underground in this complex. When they got to the Op Center, they were met by Mr. Black and Mr. Brown. As usual, they were in the black suits sans the sunglasses. They looked like they just stepped out of a Brooks Brothers catalogue, but were a bit friendlier to the rest of the team. Achilles greeted them with Honcho, and they entered into the center. The nerve center was huge, screens that would rival any others in the nation. This was huge compared to what they had at the DELTA complex at Fort Bragg. Number 1 was there, and that is when they were introduced to the Madam. She was a lady of around 50, but could easily be mistaken for 35. Honcho did the introductions, told them they would have some time to get to know each other as the unit became more operational, and they should refer to her simply as Madam or Ma'am. She joked, "I'm just an old spook from the CIA that this damn General won't let retire until I hit 80!"

Moon began by giving her the pertinent information. "Madam, we need to find a National Guard soldier who is also a Federal Agent with ICE. He should be located somewhere close to downtown Indianapolis." Madam made a quick mental note, sat down at her computer and within 10 seconds said, "I have him. Eric Lyons, yes, I have his location via the GPS tracker in his Government vehicle. He is located at the City County building, that is as long as he is where his GOV (Government Vehicle) is located.

Moon stepped up. "Honcho, I can get him on the horn, tell him I'm in town, and we could snatch him up, brief him, and see if he wants to be part of what we have going on here. He never wanted to get out of the Group, but our hard ass CO gave him shit about his weight. He played football, and is built like a rock, he just had trouble with height and weight and the bullshit way that the Army does things."

Madam let out a slow sigh. "This guy is a badass, 18D, 300 physical fitness score, has won a few Mixed Martial Arts tournaments, been to Malaysian Man hunter school, what dumbass made this man want to get out, no wonder that CBP swooped him up! And to go a step further, as an ICE agent this guy could track a mouse though a cornfield."

After a minute or two of conferring with Honcho, Madam got out a Blackberry, and gave it to Moon. Then Honcho told him, "Be vague, but let him know you are in town and have some VIP's that you want him to meet." With that , Moon dialed his old friend up, and when the phone was answered Moon said something that made them all laugh. "Hogballz, you lazy som-bitch, what the hell is going on?" Moon did some explaining, said he was with some people that wanted to meet Lyons, and that they would be up there in about 30 mikes. This made perfect sense to the ICE agent, Moon was always one for the grandeur in the time that he had known him. After another quick call Honcho contacted Lyons's boss and did a quick explanation, gave him a few codes, and told him that Lyons was on call for immediate transfer. He went onto explain that there would be an email from the NSA, and that the move might or might not be permanent. Moon reiterated that Lyons' boss was not to tell anyone what was going on, only that his agent was on a special detail.

The Blackhawk flight was quick and to the point. They met Officer Lyons at the Helipad in Downtown Indy, there they were met by another man that Honcho referred to as Mr. Yellow. He was Asian and that made Achilles and Moon laugh at least a little, and of course a Black Suburban SUV. Inside the vehicle the Doc, Honcho, Achilles, Moon and Lyons were whisked away to a silent parking garage in downtown Indy. They went in, and Mr. Yellow took them to a door in the basement of the garage. Honcho told everyone to follow him, and once inside the door Moon noticed they were in a holding cell. It was a small complex, three rooms, or one room and two cells, and what looked to be interrogation equipment. Lyons blew out his breath, said "damn McShea, what's with the cloak and dagger, and Sir, aren't you the Chairman or one of the Joint Chiefs?" Honcho reassured him. "Everything will be explained shortly, Officer Lyons, have a seat and we will go over it."

After about a half hour briefing, Lyons had all his questions answered. Honcho finished up by telling him, "Look Eric, we are going to put you on Active duty, you report to me, or Achilles here, then me, then the President. No hard ass CO bitching about height and weight, no more National Guard duty, and more pro-pays than you could ever imagine. We are set to go for an op in 24 hours, and since Moon here has vouched for you, you are in. Besides, your skill set is just what we need to round out the team. You will have to leave your life behind, your retirement will be from CBP and the Army, and you can serve until you are unable to serve any longer. I know that this is fast, but we are time sensitive, and we need a yes or no answer in the next five minutes.

"Well," Lyons said, "I got divorced last year, and I think that this is going to be fun. Not too sure I believe all this time travel shit, but Sir, I am with you. I will need to talk to my boss at CBP..." At this point he was halted and told that it was already taken care of, signed off by the President himself less than an hour ago. With that, he shook Honcho's hand, and joined the team.

Less than an hour later, they were back at the facility, and Lyons was being introduced to the rest of the team. Meat and Hollywood had already gotten all of his gear for him, most of the clothes fit, and some adjustments were made by Tinker. His pack was basically an aid station. By this time it was 1100 hours. Honcho told them all to meet at the Mess in 15 mikes and to show Lyons to the room that they were staying in. Lunch was almost a personal affair for the team. Honcho, Madam, Number 1, and the team of now five.

"First things first, CW5 Lyons, we use no rank here," said Honcho. "We go by call signs, I guess that Moon filled you in on that. With that being said, I guess you may or may not have picked a call sign?"

"Sir, I will go by Opie, a childhood nickname, and one that I answer too without thought."

The rest of the details were laid out, command structure, mission, everything that the rest of the team had already been briefed on. Honcho told everyone that the Op was a go for 1000 hours the next day, and that the team was all Achilles' to handle for the remainder of the day. They were to meet back here for a briefing and chow at 1730 hrs. With that Honcho told them they were dismissed and that he and Number 1 had things to attend to at the Op Center.

On the way out, Hollywood asked a simple question. "Sir, what is this place called? I mean we are here and we have no clue as to what to call it?" Honcho grinned and said "Oh, I never told you guys, this is what we refer to as Mid-West Control, one of the five places that all the Ass and Brass can go if the shit hits the fan."

The rest of the afternoon was spent cross-loading gear, going over small squad tactics, radio frequencies, practice with the PAD communication system, the backup commo and throat mics, and just getting to know one another. Small jokes were exchanged; it was a loose atmosphere, and to Achilles' great relief, all of these guys were as experienced or more experienced in small group tactics, anti-terrorism, and generally being bad asses than he could ever have expected. His team consisted of a Physician's Assistant, a Demo Expert, an Explosive Ordinance Disposal, Snipers, Shooters, a Communications Expert, and a Pilot rated in everything from small helicopters to dual engine airplanes. This was one kick ass group of soldiers. Even if time travel didn't work out, they were now part of something bigger and better. They could do any kind of Black Ops mission that the Government assigned them, and do it perfectly.

Dinner was served right on time, 1730. They had some good food that had been prepared and Honcho was eating left over pizza from the night before. Everyone sat around, enjoyed the meal, and were then told to enjoy the rest of the evening. Tomorrow would be a historic day, and Honcho wanted everyone prepped and ready to rock and roll for their first jump. They would be making two jumps in total, well actually four, two forward and two back. The hard one would be jumping back 3 years. They had been briefed earlier that it was impossible, but Honcho knew it was a calculated risk. This is one thing that they had all been told was going to happen, but none of them had brought it back up. The limitations were within the limits of what had been tested, but there would be no more jumps prior to 72 hours after the test. This was ordered by the Commander in Chief himself.

The rest of the evening was spent checking weapons and gear, getting comfortable and more time for the 5-man team to bond. This was one thing that Achilles was glad to have, time to get to know one another, whether it was cards, games, or just shooting the breeze, things like this were important to small unit cohesion. The one good thing was that they all had great amounts of operational experience. This would be key if thing went bad for them after a jump. No one expected trouble, but it was always great for a soldier to be prepared for the worse. As one wise man had said, all well laid plans go to shit right after an operation begins, and even though Achilles had no clue as to what lay ahead of him and his team, it was certain to be one hell of a ride.

At 0630, the sound of the alarm from Honcho's watch went off. All five men and Honcho got up, stretched and got ready for the day to come. Same as the day prior, it was chow at 0730, equipment check at 0830, and then the briefing to find out what the rest of the day had in store at 1000 hrs. Opie and Moon went to check out the gym prior to chow; the rest of the team took their time, left the stubble on their faces, and got dressed and ready. The team reconvened at the chow hall at 0830 hrs. Everyone sat and then Hollywood came up with a good question. "What if we go through this Jump, Worm Hole, or whatever and end up tossing our cookies on the other side? I mean, it had been mice and chimps so far, and they may have gotten sick, did anyone ask the White Coats about that?" Honcho gave a hearty laugh. "Well son, they came through alright, and so far as we know none of them tossed their so-called cookies after the jump." "Hopefully we don't get sick," is all that Hollywood said in response.

The team got back to their room, 113B, and everyone checked and rechecked their gear. This was something that Special Operators did on a daily basis, everything loaded, checked and re-checked.

At that moment in came Tinker. He had five watches with

him. "Gentlemen, I have got these five Suunto watches to issue out, compliments of Number 1. They have all the basics, compass, barometer, weather, temperature, stop watch, and a Universal setting that will sync up with the World clock within 30 seconds. This will give you the correct date and time wherever you jump to in the future or past. There is also a geo-locator. This can sync up to any of the six Pads that you and Honcho have. They are world-wide locator devices, so none of you can get too lost on one of these missions." Tinker looked around the group and concluded by saying, "See all of you guys at the briefing. Today is going to be super exciting, hope that it all works out and we have a go for future operations. Can't wait to get to the new location, but Honcho will go over that in the briefing later on."

At 1000 hours the team was set and ready to go. They went to the Op Center and met with Mr. Black. He escorted them into the auditorium. "This place just baffles me," said Meat, "You would never have known they had an auditorium this big underground." There were already around thirty people seated in the first couple of rows.

Right on cue at 1000 hours, Honcho entered the Auditorium. "OK everyone, I just talked to Eagle, Project Dark-Star is now a go. From this point on Seeker Element is now officially and un-officially on the books and approved by the appropriate authorities. We will have the first jump at 1300 hrs. This will be a simple 1 day reverse jump, we all know that it will happen. Madam will have a note that was written on her hand, since she and I know they are coming through, and the note will be there for everyone to see proof that it happened. After that, we will take 1 hour and do vitals, all the work ups, then do a 1 day jump back to present time. This will take place as if our team has gone and come back within one minute. At that point everyone will remember what has happened and there will be no surprises. After that, we will take another reading, then go forward with a 3 day jump. The team will not return for a few hours, we will do the same checks and balances and calibration of all the gear, then send them back. So what will feel like around 4 hours for our team, will feel crazy for the rest of us. This will be the same as last time with the chimp, and also the time before with the mice. It is going to be a monumental day, so everyone keep your shit straight and let's make some history!" That got the crowd clapping and ready to go. Honcho dismissed everyone except for the Seeker Element.

"Gentlemen," he said. "If the shit hits the fan, you are to rally in one of five government facilities. There is here of course, Cheyenne Mountain in Colorado, Area-51, Langley, or the other location that we have kept relatively secret until now. We have a facility here in Indianapolis. It is at the DFAS location at the former Fort Harrison. I am sure that Opie knows where I am talking about. Just keep going down and there should be someone to direct you if you get lost. No matter what, your PADS and trackers will work, your info is in the system and anyone who is in charge if everything goes awry will be able to confirm everything. You are by no means to be debriefed by anyone that isn't wearing the rank of 3 Stars or above. On your Pads there are personnel records so that you can verify anything that needs verifying. This is just one of those no shit things that I like to tell operatives before a mission. The only real concerning jump won't happen until the 3rd jump, which is the 3 year jump anyway. I just like to be prepared and ready for anything that can happen to my people. Are there any questions?"

At this point no one asked any questions, and Honcho dismissed the team. He asked for Achilles and Meat to stay behind for a moment. "Guys, I just want you to know that this all is a little in the uncharted territory, you have handled yourselves well and look like you are ready to get it done. I need a no shit answer, are we good to go?" Both on cue knew the answer and sounded off with "Good to go Sir." With that, Honcho shook their hands, and told them to be ready and back in the main hanger at quarter till 1300. They walked back to 113B, where everyone was doing some last second type things such as weapons checks, safeties, dry fire weapons checks, and then came what was another great question. This one was from Opie. "Hey Achilles," he said, "When are we going to test fire and zero these weapons?" That was another no brainer, they walked over with their gear on and ready to go to the Supply/Arms room, and Tinker was there as usual.

"Tink," Achilles asked, "is there a range in here?"

"Sure is, almost thought about bringing that up last night, but decided you guys knew what you were doing. It's just the next room over, sound proof, and there is a 500 meter target even." Tinker jerked his thumb over his shoulder towards the range.

They walked into the adjoining room, donned some ear and eye protection, loaded up some practice ammo and spent the next hour zeroing and basically firing every weapon that they had. After that they spent time cleaning and getting their weapons ready to go. They then mounted up and went to the hanger 15 mikes before show time. Honcho was there with a smile on his face and told Madam that he had won the bet, which was basically how early they would show up. Madam had from 1 to 14:49 minutes, and Honcho had the rest. They were there 15:31 prior to show time, almost right on cue for Honcho's gut feeling. The bottom line, they were all professionals, and that is the way that these types of Operators acted. Ready to go at a moment's notice, on time and early when needed.

15 minutes prior to jump time they were screened, vitals taken, locaters on and in the green, com checks initiated, everything synced and ready to go. Number 1 and the Doc were at the control center, and just like Hollywood had said, there was what looked every bit of a Star-gate. He made a sound and said, "Just like the movies. If only we could slip our arm through some mercury-type material and make it look all good like in the movies,

ha-ha." Number 1 told them to expect anything, there would be intense light from the gate, and that they should feel maybe a quick falling sensation or possibly a little bit of vertigo. It should be instantaneous and they would arrive back exactly one day prior. Power was brought online, Honcho stood 20 feet away wearing goggles, the team had their Oakleys on and said a final few words to Honcho. With that they got the green light from the top of the Gate, Honcho told them "God Speed," just like what was said to John Glenn a half century before. They approached the gate and entered what looked like a lightning storm. Less than 10 seconds later they walked right out into the hanger with the group waiting on them.

When they came through, Meat puked his breakfast on cue, Opie stumbled a bit and they all looked green and ready to get sick. Medical teams were there, gear was handed off, and Honcho had a huge shit eating grim on his face. "What do we eat for breakfast in the morning?" was his first question to the team. Achilles held up a finger, asked him not to mention food for a while, and they all took their seat on the gurneys that were sitting there for them. Medical checks were performed, more than they were expecting, and they were all good to go within 15 minutes of the first jump. Honcho just kept grinning, all the scientists were patting each other on the backs, everything seemed to be A-OK. With that the time to go back was upon them. The gate was re-fired up, and they went back to the day they had just come from. The jump was the same, they all had the queasiness and felt a little sick, but the teams were there to attend to them.

Medical checks and exams were a bit more extensive, this time they went to the infirmary, had blood taken and had to do all the routine checks of a physical. The entire team was good to go, Meat even pulled some food out of his pack that the rest of the team was snacking on. At that point Honcho and Number 1 came into the room. "Gentlemen," Honcho said, "are you ready to make a little more history today, or do we wait for tomorrow to finish this little experiment?" They all looked at one another, gave the thumbs up, and Achilles said "Looks like we are a go at this time Sir, let's get it done!" After a small brief, in which they were told that they would be sent ahead again but this time 36 months into the future, where people would be waiting, data would be checked, uploaded to their Pads. They would then be sent back to the present, about 1 minute after their initial leave time. They got their gear on, did a final check and were escorted back to the hanger with Honcho, Number 1 and or course Mr. Black.

"OK everyone," Number 1 said, "the clock is set, the flux capacitor is ready to go." That got a chuckle from the entire group. Moon said "OK Dr. Brown, send us back to the future," and everyone busted up and was a little less uptight. "One last thing," came from Honcho. "I have complete authority on this, no one but me will be in charge when you come back, short of my dying. If that happens my replacement will know what to do, he is briefed and knows the drill. If I am dead in the future, I am not to be told that when you guys come back, is that understood?" The entire group gave a chorus of Hoo-ah's and they waited on the green light once again. The machine spun up, taking a little while longer this time, Number 1 told them it was because it was for a longer jump, and that they would see them in 3 years. "Oh yeah," added Tink, "if you find out that the Cubs have won the World Series, you know then that the experiment went way wrong!" This got a chuckle out of Achilles and a few others. Number 1 said that he would see them in a few .... years, and everyone got ready to go. The lightning storm in the gate looked the same to anyone watching, intense and like something from an experiment gone bad, the team one by one shook Honcho's hand, and walked up the ramp. One last salute from Achilles and the team stepped into the storm. Time and date check, 28 Jun 2010, 1900 hrs.

What had before seemed like only seconds seemed like

forever for the team. They were experiencing time dementia, or something like it. After what seemed to be an eternity they walked out of the gate.

CHAPTER 4
2013

When the team emerged, there was no one to greet them. No one to help them with the nausea, no one to administer medical checks, only a hanger with dust and abandoned equipment. This was the 'no shit' scenario that they had talked about, problems that were beyond belief and a reality that there was no one to send them back. On shaky legs and sour stomachs Achilles gave the order for a defensive perimeter. They took a few minutes to perform a sight and sound check, and their atomic watches synced up. 28 Jun 2013, 1901 hrs. That was concerning, they were at the jump gate, right on target and no one was there to greet them.

"OK guys," Achilles said, "let's get some com's up, recon the area in 2 man teams, Meat with me, Opie and Moon check out the Op center and 113B, Hollywood, stay here and try to raise someone on the PAD. No, scratch that, Moon you stay, Wood you go with Opie and see what you can find." The two teams set out, checked in via com patch through the PADS, and went their separate ways. Achilles and Meat checked the main hanger. There was a Suburban with no keys, probably a long dead battery since the dome light would not even illuminate; they didn't bother with the horn. All the equipment was covered in plastic, and there was nothing else to be found. They then went into the supply room, rifle mounted flashlights on and surveyed the interior. Everything was boxed up and gone. There was nothing left, only dust and dirt filled the area. They left the supply room and returned to the jump gate only to find out that Moon had had no luck raising anyone on the radio, there was no internet feed to find, nothing.

Hollywood and Opie started down the long hallway leading to 113B, did a quick scan of the area, checked to see if there was power. The lights came on, and even the water ran. The water worked in the latrine. They took note and went on down the hallway that was lit under emergency lighting. They made their way to the Op center, the only problem was that there was a card reader that secured the door. That shouldn't be a problem considering the equipment that they were carrying, and the fact that Moon was a bit of a hacker. They looked around, most of the doors were secure, and basically the facility seemed to be a ghost town. They went back toward the main hanger, and linked back up with the rest of the team. Moon was still having no luck in trying to reach anyone. They were back together and all feeling the ill effects of the jump. The hanger was essentially secure, no door was open, and as far as they could tell the active camouflage was still working. That was one bit of good news, this facility also had its own power source, Nuclear or Solar, no one knew, but they thought it was Nuclear since the power needed for the gate was probably a lot.

After a few minutes of trying to get their bearings and get over the post-effects of the jump, the nausea and the falling feeling were starting to wear away. A meeting was what was needed. Achilles started with a simple question. "What the hell happened, they had done this with the chimp and the mice, and where the fuck are the people that were supposed to be here waiting on us?" Moon had an idea. "Maybe we look around and try to get into the Op center. I have the tool kit and access codes, and think that we should be able to get in. Once inside, we can try to establish better com's, and going outside without assessing the situation may be a bad idea." Hollywood said he felt the same, if something bad had transpired, they might need to gather intelligence and try to figure out their next move. Everyone seemed to think that was a great idea, they gathered their stuff, and got up to move. A split second later they heard a noise from the normal sized door that was connected to the main hangar door. They all dropped into a crouch, Achilles held up his fist to signify everyone to freeze. Weapons were trained toward the sound, the main problem was that there was not that much light, and no one had their night vision out or attached to their helmets.

And out of the dark appeared just a single person, dirty and carrying a dead deer in a fireman's carry over his shoulder, rifle slung over his shoulder, and a sidearm on his hip. About 20 feet from the team he looked up and stopped in mid stride. "Holy shit, it worked!" he gasped in amazement. It was Tinker, he was there and maybe, just maybe had some answers.

"Tink, where is everyone? What the fuck is going on? Why do you look like a hitchhiker?" All the questions came like shotgun blasts, while Tinker just stood there in disbelief. Then he actually broke down and started crying, dropped the doe, and ran up and actually hugged Achilles, then Moon, Meat, Hollywood, and finally Opie. "Man. you guys are really here! It's amazing, we thought you were gone, but of course we would have, we wouldn't have seen you until now, actually 30 minutes ago to be exact, I can't believe I am such a bone head that I didn't have an alarm set for this. No, no alarm, sound can be bad. You guys really have a lot to take in, I am going to tell you everything, everything. Honcho told me to stay, to remain behind, to stockpile and keep everything in order just in case we were able to hold out." He sniffed and wiped his arm across his eyes.

"Slow down, Tinker," Achilles said gently, "there is plenty of time, take it easy, how long since you have heard from anyone else? How long have you been here yourself?"

"It's been about 19 months, since the flu, since the outbreak, been 18 months since the Day of Reckoning as some of the other people I have spoken to have called it. There isn't much news, things are broken. Let's get this deer to the galley, then we can go to the Op center and I can give you guys a complete rundown on it all. I have kept a journal, and most of the computer systems have stored data. I haven't been in contact with Honcho since about 90 days after the blasts, the Satellite communications and cell, well, come one, I will show you guys and give you a proper briefing. I'm no General, but as a Sergeant First Class and the supply officer, I think I can get it done."

Tinker led them back down the long hall, explained that most of the power to things was shut off to conserve the nuclear reactor. "Running at full capacity, this place can stay operational for 20 years, kind of like an aircraft carrier, but at minimum power it could be more like 100 years. I just use what I need, and try to keep everything in working order. Not too shabby if I do say so myself," he said proudly.

They got to the Op Center, where Tinker slipped in his CAC card. All of them had them, but Tink explained that theirs would need to be reprogrammed to gain access, no worries, he would take care of it. They entered the Op Center, Tinker flipped a switch, and lights and terminals came to life. In 30 seconds the place was lit up like it had been for the team less than a day prior.

Tinker sat down at the briefing table, this was the same 6 foot long oak table they had sat at 3 years ago. The last time they saw it, it had been covered with papers, briefing folders and Madam's purse. Now it was bare. Tinker told them what would be a short version of a very long story....

"Well, we sent you guys through the gate, and everyone basically put this facility into mothballs. It was originally meant to be a last stand type place for Congressmen, Senators, High Brass

Military Types, State and Federal Officials, and those types. This place is huge, you guys only got to see bits and pieces. The operation was progressing so fast, Honcho put things into overdrive. You guys happened to be at Walter Reed, Opie, you came into the picture and fit into the team well. Everyone was happy and things appeared to go just as planned. Then I was appointed to be the NCOIC of the place, to keep it maintained, and to basically be the caretaker. Everyone planned to come back a day prior to your jump, get things working and then send you back. That would have been the plan, just as we all briefed it. Except that on December 12th 2011, word was sent out via official channels that there was an outbreak in North Korea. Some sort of strain of the Bird Flu seemed to be killing the peasants. This wasn't the bad part, the official reports were that the dead started to come back, they were turning into something that unofficially was referred to as Zombies!"

"Hold on there Tink, zombies, what the hell is going on here?" Meat seemed to have had enough. "This is some kind of joke, where is Honcho and when is this masquerade going to be over with?"

Tink shook his head solemnly. "No joke, guys, if you will let me finish, Sir, I will show you all the data that your heart desires. Do you really think that a place like this would be in this kind of condition if something major hadn't occurred out there?" That really made a lot of sense to the team, and Achilles told him to continue. "Well, after a week, people and pictures started to come out of North Korea, aid was sent via the United Nations, Honcho had to stay in D.C. and go through briefings and meetings about what to do. He contacted me via our secure data link, told me that if the shit did hit the fan, that if things got worse, the entire hierarchy would be at Cheyenne Mountain. Anyway, the UN Security Council held emergency meetings, China was even included. The decision to nuke North and South Korea came in less than an hour of their debate. The DMZ (demilitarized zone) had been overrun by these Zombie reanimated things. All of the remaining soldiers and what not from the US military had to stay, hell, they didn't even get alerted about the nuke. The decision that letting them know would only cause alarm and cause them to flee, that would only help what was later known as the T-68 Strain jump from the Korean Peninsula and transfer the flu to mainland China, and possibly to the rest of the world."

"The decision came. The world was alerted when the missiles were launched. That is what I am referring to as the Day of Reckoning. Before we knew it, North Korea launched their own, all those missile tests, all the fear that they had nuclear capabilities, it was all true. Next thing you know, we are in nuclear fallout. All the major cities and ports were danger zones. The radiation and fallout is like Chernobyl on crack. It's only been a few years, but that isn't the bad part. The infection had jumped; within days of the bombs there were zombies everywhere. The infected ones spread it by biting or scratching the living. There is no cure, no way to get rid of it. I had contact with Cheyenne for about 6 months, then the satellites were no longer online. Email is down, cell phones are shit, I have been waiting here to see if you guys made it just like I was ordered. I was told that there would be relief, but none ever came. I thought about going to Indy, but it's a danger zone. Large cities are full of 'walkers' as I've started to call them. They don't die, they just multiply by killing the living. They just seem to stand around, to wait, to be in some kind of zone, and then when there is sound, they come swarming. I have cameras that look around the post. There aren't many here, most of the guard got mobilized and within weeks they were shattered. The military tried to eradicate the walkers, but then the runners came. They were like the walkers, only they had been exposed to the fallout, this caused another transmutation and they seem to be faster and smarter.

"Guys, I know that this is a lot to sink in, it has been a busy few days for you, just think about this, I have lived this nightmare for 19 months! I have been alone and out of contact. The world is like Mad Max's world out there. There are automated defenses here, but the active camo seems to keep them away from here. I only go out and hunt when I can't take anymore MRE's or C-Rations. That's why I went out and got a deer today. I guess in the back of my mind, if I can still catch and eat wild game, I am doing something for my survival. I have been alone, and basically felt like I was the only one left for such a long time."

The team took the time to go through the records. It was the way that Tinker had said. There was no way to communicate. Vehicle travel seemed to be done; there were no flights going anywhere. There was no way to communicate any farther than 20 to 30 miles. So, after all the reading, all the moments of shock and awe, the news that was at this point 18 months old had just started to sink into the minds of the team. The only break was the fact that Opie looked at Moon and said, "Why me mother fucker! I could have been in my own world and ended up a Zombie!" They all laughed, Moon then said, "Join the Army!" They all repeated in unison, "See the world," and they laughed.

Around 0030 hours Achilles had enough of the news and information. They needed to sleep, regroup, eat, and try to figure out their next plan of action. They all decided to go to the friendly confines of 113B. Tinker set the silent alarm, had the place buttoned up tight, and assured them all that there would be no one getting in or out without them knowing about it. Strange as it may sound, this was going to be one of the best nights of sleep that they all would get for a long time. They had just found out that the world had ended, that their careers, families, friends, and nation were all just long gone memories. They went to sleep, all silently thinking that they would wake up and it would all just be a bad dream.

The next morning came fast. Hollywood was up and

cleaning up when the rest of the team started to rise. He had opened the door and everyone could smell the sweet barbecue that was being cooked by Tinker. They got up, cleaned up, loaded their gear and headed for the mess. No one really spoke, the only thing that was said was by Meat. "Are we still in Thunderdome?" This got a few laughs by the group. Achilles thought to himself that if they still had any sense of humor that it was pretty good, and morale wasn't as bad as he thought. By that time breakfast was ready, barbecued venison, powdered eggs, concentrate orange juice, and even hot coffee. They all sat down, thanked Tinker for making breakfast and started to strategize about what to do next.

Achilles began. "Well, basically men I see a few choices. We can try to stay here and wait for reinforcements, but that could be some time down the line. Tink has been here for quite some time and he has had no contact. We can requisition a vehicle, store what we need, head west for Cheyenne Mountain and take it as it comes our way." They all mulled it over.

"Tink, how have you been getting around out there?" Achilles asked.

"Oh, I use a modified ATV from the motor pool, you may have used them before, they're almost silent. Oh yeah, and I never clean my body off unless I itch really bad or get any of their blood on me. That stuff will turn you in a heartbeat, kind of like getting prepared for Saudi and doing all that decontamination stuff. Their sense of smell is incredible, so I usually go au natural. And all of the vehicles are in working order, batteries are charged, ready to go, you also may be surprised at what is here, in a post apocalypse world, I can't think of any better place to end up," Tink finished his report.

The team didn't need a lot of time to think it over. Get to Cheyenne, reestablish contact with their command, and then do what was needed to be done and make everything normal again. Maybe if Honcho and some of the scientists were around, they would have a plan to make the world right again.

Achilles turned to Tink again. "Tink, what in the way of transportation can we sign for to get on our way? And are you going to come with us?"

Tink thought about it for a moment and then said, "Well, you have your choice of just about anything. There are some great armored Stryker vehicles, they can be sealed for NBC environments, and might be your best choice. They also have been retrofit and run off of basically any kind of fuel that you can find."

They took a walk to the motor pool. Tinker had been right, there was just about everything from ATV's, Motorbikes, Hummers, Range Rovers, Pick-ups, even an M1 tank. The Stryker was the obvious choice. They would need to plan a route. Since GPS was down, they would have to use map and compass, but they were all trained at navigating this way. The Stryker had a 30 MM cannon on top, this would be great for crowd control. They would need some time to get everything loaded up and ready to move.

The team spent the next few hours loading gear, surplus fuel, water and food, and even batteries. Tink had thought of everything that they might need. He made the comment that he had thought about making the trip alone, but he knew that waiting for the team was the right move. At that point Tink told Achilles that he was staying behind. This was now his home, his duty station, and he would keep it secure for as long as needed. Hollywood came up with a few routes, all avoiding populated areas, and no town bigger than 50,000 or so people. They would even skirt those with as wide of a berth as possible. They got siphon material and made a final check of the vehicle. Spare tires were mounted to the rear of the vehicle, and they all got in and loaded up. Next stop, wherever they ran into trouble or Cheyenne Mountain, whichever came first.

CHAPTER 5
THE ROAD

The team got ready to set out in the modified version of the Army's Stryker armored transport vehicle. The route that they had decided upon would take them at least 50 miles around any large city like Indianapolis. Their route would take them back roads, state highways, and then major highways depending upon fuel, abandoned vehicles, and other obstacles. According to, there was everything from walkers, runners, to bandits out in the open. His description was that the United States had returned to almost a Wild West type of atmosphere; every man was armed and more likely to shoot first and ask questions later. He knew this from the news that was still being broadcast while networks and other forms of media were still available.

Hollywood spoke to the group about taking a Blackhawk, but maintenance, fuel and other issues made it a bad choice. Tink had told them what he knew about the undead, that sound attracted them, and that they were more docile during the day. They seemed to mill about slowly as if in a state of sleep. That was good since the Stryker was a bit loud, and they planned to move during daylight hours at this point anyway. Moon took up running the electronics, trying to get someone on coms. Hollywood would ridge as the gunner, he could control the 30mm that was on top.

They also had picked up a few M-240's and a .50 caliber that was mounted up top. If there was ever a group ready to go out into this wasteland, Achilles swore that they couldn't be any better than the group that he had under his command.

The first step was getting off of Camp Atterbury; there were both walkers and runners that Tink had run into. He told the group that he would hunt when necessary, but only during daylight hours. The best bet was to try to avoid and outrun the undead, that way they would blindly follow sound (and possibly smell) until they lost range of it. Tink told them that he thought that they could smell him, that was why he was in such a state of uncleanliness when they found him. So with all of that in mind, they were going to head off of post, head west and start the long trek towards Colorado and Cheyenne Mountain. The current plan was to first head to Terre Haute, a smaller college town that was the former site of Indiana State University, then try to make their way north and west toward I-70. The first day the plan was to make it as far as Terre Haute. That would put them close to the border of Illinois, and well on their way.

They said their goodbyes to Tink, and he wished them luck. Then they left the hangar and set a course which would take them near the airfield, then off of the base via the most direct route. Everyone was a little on edge, and the fact that they would be entering basically a wasteland made everyone put their game faces on. They used the Internal Communications System or ICS, that way they could save the batteries on the PADS and backup come. Everyone was locked and loaded and ready to go.

After turning on the main road to the exit post Meat stopped the vehicle. There was the first contact, two walkers standing in the middle of the road. "Boss, how do you want me handle this?" asked Hollywood. Without missing a beat, Achilles told him to handle it quietly. That was all that was needed, everyone knew that this meant suppressors. "Hollywood," Achilles said, "try to conserve and go for head shots." That seemed to be what worked best from the little bit of Intel that they had gathered via the archived news at the Hangar. With that Meat moved the Stryker forward at a snail's pace, and the two walkers moved toward the vehicle. Hollywood put two well-aimed shots in between the eyes of both of the walkers; they dropped. "Looks like this may be slow going," said Opie. He was looking for contacts with Hollywood, more of the walkers were coming out from in between buildings and from behind abandoned vehicles.

"Meat, gun it!" said Achilles. "Hold on to your asses, boys, we're bugging out."

It was relatively easy to get around the walkers, the next problem would be the gate, it was sealed up tight, and that could also be an issue. "Boss, I could just try to ram it, or we could blow it off of its hinges with the cannon?" Meat speculated. That was a good thought, getting out of here and on the road was the best option, they needed to get moving and try to put some distance between them and these things. Just then Moon came across the ICS and told them that maybe skirting the fence line could provide them with an exit. "Great idea," said Achilles, "but what do you guys think of blowing it, maybe hurry up there and place some C-4 on the gate? That may bring some to us, but we can blow it and maybe that will pull some away from this location and provide Tink with a little easier hunting?" Everyone gave a good to go. Hollywood made great time, swerved in and out through the walkers and they made it to the gate. Opie jumped out, placed some C-4 on the hinges, inserted blasting caps and made his way back inside with at least 30 meters to spare between him and any walkers. When he stepped into the hatch and secured it, Hollywood let everyone know that there were more coming, and they appeared to be running and not walking. Achilles made a command decision. "Take'em out, get that .50 rocking and rolling!" Hollywood went to work mowing down adversaries, and Meat opened the hatch and put two well-aimed shots in the C-4. The gate exploded off of its hinges. "Get us out of here Meat!" Achilles shouted over the ICS, and with that Meat gunned it and pushed the gate out of the way. It was about another 50 yard drive, and then they turned west toward the town of Trafalgar.

At least that turned out OK for the team. The road seemed to be deserted, no cars on the shoulder, and nothing following them. They spoke to Tink and he advised that they would be out of contact in a few hours, but thanked the team for the distraction. It would keep the undead farther away from the Hangar and make it easier for him to get some fresh game. "Speaking of that Tink," Moon said over the radio, "I was thinking about that deer we ate with you, any chance that they could have contracted whatever made these zombies?" It was a simple answer, they were told that it seemed to only affect the humans at this point, and that there was some news that it also affected some forms of primates such as chimps and monkeys. Nothing more had been heard out of the CDC since Atlanta had been turned into a nuclear wasteland.

Here it was 1600 hours, it would be dark in around four hours and they were on the road making good time. Meat was cruising about 35 mph, and heading due west. Moon came up with an idea. "Hollywood, what are the frequencies for GUARD on UHF and VHF? We could broadcast and try to reach someone, those radios reach farther than FM, and if we broadcast like that we can at least see if anyone has their ears on out there." Hollywood responded "UHF is 243.0, and VHF is 121.5." "Man," said Opie, "great idea you geek!" Those two always seemed to rib one another, but knowing each other for a long time, then keeping up with each other made them pretty tight. Achilles would keep that in mind if they had to split up for anything that came up during the movement that they were on.

Moon's broadcast was simple, effective and in the blind. Before he did put it out there he asked Achilles what call sign he should use. "At this point I would be vague, let's not use seeker or any other Military call sign, just try to sound like a civilian, and maybe we can find someone out there to figure out our situation." Moon broadcast and all that came back was a little static, nothing more. "OK Moon, just keep trying every 15 mikes, maybe someone out there still uses radios to communicate, if there is any Military to speak of we might be able to rendezvous and let them give us the skinny about what is going on these days."

With that they kept heading west. They should be around the next turn in about 10 mikes or so according to their estimates and maps that they had in their PADS. Moon spoke up, "Man, if GPS worked still we could track where we are heading and have it easy, but as you guys know, easy isn't the way that it ever is!" They came to an intersection where there was an abandoned gas station and a few stores including a Burger King. They all looked as if they had seen better days. "OK Meat," Achilles warned, "let's make it through town and get back on the open road as soon as we can."

Moving through the town was like something out of a movie. Long abandoned cars, trucks, and trash were everywhere. At least the road was somewhat clear, people were definitely still eking out survival, but they weren't showing themselves if they were here in town. Meat drove and weaved in and out of obstacles. Hollywood and Achilles could see walkers. They'd watch them turn and look towards the noise, then start shambling after the Stryker. The place felt just wrong to the entire team: A town that looked deserted, walkers milling about and making their way to the sound of the vehicle. Fortunately this town was small, it came and went and they got on down the road without a shot being fired. It was interesting to say the least. They were all talking over the ICS wondering if there were larger groups, and about the best way to avoid them and make it to Cheyenne Mountain with as little contact as possible.

Moon made the comment that they should make a map, maybe keep a running journal of the contacts that they saw, the conditions of towns and such, and that maybe this would provide whatever was left of the government with some vital Intel that they could use. Another great idea, from the previously retired Command Sergeants Major.

Their route would take them next through some other "stop light" type towns, and then they could head more toward I-70 and get on the highway. It was approaching 1900 hours and by their estimation they would be another 30 mikes from hitting I-70. They could cut through corn fields, it was dry out and they had an all-terrain vehicle, but maybe sticking to the paved roads would provide the path of least resistance. The Stryker had around a 300 mile range at a good pace, and they would do what they could to milk it. The next step would be to find some fuel and the Interstate. Achilles and the team talked about this. Fuel would be the first issue that they would have to deal with, then water, then food. At least they weren't on foot, they hadn't run across a large mass of the undead, and they were armed and semi ready for whatever they would run across.

Nighttime was approaching fast. Achilles' first thought was pull off of the road, button up tight, and try to get some shut eye. They would pull the standard two hour security at twenty percent, monitor the scope and see if anything came at them. They had the luxury of being able to stay inside, and the security of a sealed environment. The only issue was if they did pull off the road, what kind of company might show up from following the Stryker and the noise that it produced, and also, possibly the smell from the engine? Those were questions that the team mulled over while cutting down a northbound road outside of Cloverdale, Indiana. They decided to keep on going for a while, to see if they could find a safe place to hunker down for the night. Meat was getting used to driving, they all would have to take turns behind the screen gunning, TC'ing, and manning the monitors. Hollywood came across the ICS and told Achilles and the rest of the team that he found what looked to be a good place to hole up. It was a sub-station for electricity, the gate was locked by a chain and there was gravel to park on. Plus it had the added benefit that the entire 100x50 complex had a fence around it. "Good thinking, Woody," Achilles said, and that was it, he would unofficially be called Woody from now on. No biggie, they all seemed to gel and handle what each other said. The real test would be if the shit really did hit the proverbial fan. Meat pulled up to the gate, Woody gave the all clear, Ope and Achilles were out with bolt cutters, and the gate to the place was open and ready to be home for the night.

Securing the gate was relatively easy, they would use a C-Clamp that was in the tool kit, along with the chain that had the lock on it. The good thing about the Stryker was that you could run the electronics for over 24 hours without having the engine cranked, that way they could monitor the outside and no one would have their noise or smell outside. They would look like a vehicle that had been sitting here all along. Achilles and the guys talked over MRE's ("Meals Ready to Eat"), and of course water to drink. They were all professionals; this was actually living the high life compared to what they had all been through while attending one special operations school or another. The engine was shut off, they were at close to 9/16th's tank of fuel, and could button up tight.

Moon kept on broadcasting in the blind. They now did it every 30 mikes, that way they could at least see if anyone else was out there in the new shit hole of a planet that they were now living in. Achilles assigned the watch. It was easy enough, they did it alphabetically by their call signs, Achilles, Hollywood, Meat, Moon, then Opie would pull the last shift. No complaints, there wasn't a ton of room in the Stryker, but there was enough room that the five of them, their gear, and the extra stuff that they took with them could afford them with some bit of comfort. They all thought about making this place ready to go dark. Everyone got out, pissed and surveyed their location under night vision. Things were quiet enough, they got back in, sealed the hatch and went to sleep.

The first three watches came and went. Achilles, Woody, and Meat didn't see a thing. There weren't even the glowing eyes of wild life creatures that one would normally see while looking through night-vision scopes or goggles. About half way through Moon's shift he was trying to monitor the radios and the scope, nothing that was too difficult to handle, when he heard the moans.

At first they were just distant muffled sounds, then the silhouettes of the walkers showed up at the fences. In the beginning there were one or two, then by the end of his shift there were five. It wasn't a big deal, they had assumed that the walkers would follow the noise. There had to be some here and there just wandering long ago plowed and planted corn and soy bean fields, but he decided to wake Achilles anyway. "Boss," he said, "we have contact." That was nothing that was out of the ordinary for this team, they had all been in and out of way worse situations and scenarios in training and in the real world missions that they had all been a part of. Achilles looked out the scope, saw what the salty Sergeant Major saw, and they both let Opie know what to expect during his watch. The three were talking quietly, discussing the situation, when Meat spoke up. "Flamethrower, boss, that's what we need, burn em up and keep gunfire quiet, and those fuckers would just burn up and never regenerate."

As the team was talking, Woody stretched and joined in the conversation. Looked like 0400 hours was the last time that anyone would be getting any shut eye. Moon went to work sending out the same broadcast into the open. "Anyone out there, I am trying to establish contact near Cloverdale, Indiana, I am broadcasting on guard, anyone out there, Over." Static, just like there had been for the last 12 hours. He thought to himself, 'It's worth a shot.' Then

Moon thought he heard a reply, so he turned up the volume and it came again. "Person broadcasting on guard, it is great to hear someone else's voice, if you can come back? Over."

"Boss!" Moon said, "we have contact."

"Hello out there, my name is Mark, I am east of Cloverdale, I am seeking contact and a situation report for the area, Over." Then he turned to Achilles and asked, "Boss, what do you want me to do? Should we try to set up contact?"

Achilles thought about it for a moment, then replied, "Sounds great Moon, see if they want to rendezvous and maybe share some information."

"Mark, my name is Kit, I sent a runner to get our leader, he will do the talking, it's been a while since we have had any contact with anyone else, are you around any of the Infected? Over."

"Kit, we have been moving west, we have had some contact, no real numbers, mostly walkers and not too many runners, what about your guys? Over."

"Mark, we have sporadic contact, but our leader can tell you about all that, he should be here in a few minutes, Over."

"Sounds good Kit, great to hear another human voice, been a while." With that, Moon rolled his eyes. The rest of the team was listening in also. "We are just trying to find some fuel and restock our water... Kit, can you guys help with that? Over."

"Hello Mark, my name is David," came a grizzly sounding voice over the radio. "I am in charge here, we haven't had any contact from anyone in a while, where about are y'all coming from? Over."

Achilles told Moon to embellish a bit. "We are coming from the East coast, been on the run now since the shit hit the fan, we are looking to refit with some diesel and water, is there any way we can link up and trade? Over."

"Mark, what is your location in reference to the Intersection of I-70 and the Cloverdale exit? Over."

"We are a few miles out, how many are with your crew David? Over."

"Not too sure if I can trust you Mark, there are bandits and thieves about these days, last time we had some human contact was a couple of months back, it was unpleasant to say the least. We are a little leery these days, Over."

"David, I am with you, not too many people that you can trust these days, could we meet up and talk about it? Over."

"Mark, we can do that, I will need to get my people ready. There is a road that leads north from Cloverdale toward a town called Greencastle. There is an intersection there. I-40, it's the Old National Road. It's on good ground, nothing but fields and a Shell Station on the corner. We can link up there are 9:00 am if you like, Over."

"David, that sounds great, we will come from the south, we look forward to meeting you guys, Over."

"Mark, come unarmed, at least that way we know that there are no shenanigans or double crossing that will be going on, we have the gas station secure. You will see men with rifles on the roof, they will watch you coming, and know if there are any guns on you. Over."

"Sounds good to me, David, 9:00 am it is, Over and Out." Moon ended the conversation with a grin and a thumbs-up to Achilles.

Chapter 6
The Greencastle Regulars

First light was around 0615, it was warm and there was dew on the ground. When the team emerged from the Stryker, there were nine walkers milling about the fence. They noticed that they had trampled the knee high grass around the fence, as if trying to find a way in. After taking pisses and a few guys doing their other business, they decided that they should put the walkers down with suppressed shots from the .45's. Hollywood and Achilles looked at their route. They would go as far as a mile from the meeting place where Meat and Achilles would disarm except for the Micro-Compact .45's that they would store on their bodies and the combat knifes that they had on their belts. Commo would run by the FM radios and throat mics that they all had. Woody would find a vantage point and cover them with the M-24, most probably a tree that he could climb. Moon and Ope would maintain security around the Stryker.

They got on the road and made their way to the rendezvous point, or at least as close as they would venture. These locals weren't the only ones worried about an ambush, this entire team had dealt with indigenous forces in back country civilizations around the world. There were always good and bad, if you didn't get shot at in the first few minutes of a meeting, then generally the people were good. At 0815 hours they were in position, set and ready to go.

They pulled the Stryker off the road next to a wood-line. The engine was cut and commo checks were made. Woody scaled a tall tree with a great vantage point where he could see the Shell Station. He was using the spotter scope to keep sunlight from glinting off of the rifle. At that point, he was glad that Tinker had insisted upon them taking some other useful items, since they were riding and not walking, it made too much sense. In this case he had the Barrett .50 cal sniper rifle with him, and had donned the Ghillie suit so that he couldn't be seen. Ope and Moon were inside and watching the scopes, they could follow the guys via the thermal scope and had a good view of the valley and the hill leading up the road to the gas station.

Moon came across. "Boss, I see the thermal signatures of five bodies, two on the roof, and it looks like three inside, two in one room, 1 possibly hidden from view upon entry, Over."

"Good to know Moon, we will keep the mics open so you guys can hear everything. Woody, do you see anything out there in between us and them? Over."

"Nothing so far, boss, looks clear, it's like Tink said, doesn't look like there is much activity during the day, don't even see any of them milling about. Our rear is still clear, I will see them coming, Over," Woody responded.

Achilles and Meat made their way up the hill, there was nothing but open fields to the east and west, there was the wood-line to the south, and past the gas station about 100 meters there was another wood-line. That gave the people they were meeting a great vantage point and the high ground. Achilles commented over the radio that he saw one of their snipers on the roof, couldn't see the other one but counted on Hollywood and Moon to keep the perspective for him and Meat. As they approached the rendezvous, they could tell that this gas station had seen better days, but looked to be fortified in the inside.

"Hello in there," Achilles said, "Anyone home?"

"That will be about far enough soldier boy." With that, out came David from the door. "We haven't seen many soldiers since after the government fell apart, and the fact that you guys look like you just raided an Army/Nave surplus store makes me wonder about you!"

"Easy there friend." responded Achilles. "We are Active duty Army, well at least we were when our mission started, we are unarmed, and just seek some updates about what you guys know is going on around these parts, maybe even a trade for some food, fuel and water. We have stuff to barter with, and if you take money we can do that also."

With that being said David laughed. "Money, what do you think this is, 2010? Ha-Ha, that is about the funniest thing that I've heard in over a year. If you are truly soldiers, raise up those shirts and do a 360 so that I can see if you are really unarmed." Meat and Achilles obliged the man. Their paddle holsters were hidden and wouldn't be seen unless they were actually patted down, the only thing showing were the two knifes that each of them were carrying. The sniper on the roof was in plain view, looked to be a woman but was wearing Ray-Ban sunglasses and a camouflaged patrol cap. David's backup, a man of around 6'2" came out and stood by his side. He was carrying an AR-15, that was a civilian model that was similar to the older models of M-16 that the Army had used forever, or at least since Vietnam.

"OK soldier boys," said David, "this is how it's going to go. I know that you aren't alone, and probably have people watching us, just like we have other people watching you. We can do this the easy way, you can come inside, we can discuss what's going on in the world, maybe even come up with some kind of deal and be all sorts of friendly with one another, or we can just shoot you, take them knives and deal with your friends. You want it that way or you can turn over those side-arms that I know you are carrying. Without doing that I can't really even begin to trust you."

"Well Mr. David," a little nicety from growing up in Savannah that Achilles always used when talking to someone in charge or older, "we can have a Mexican Stand-off out here and just talk from where we are, or we can keep these side-arms and let your man keep us covered while we talk. It's way too dangerous with those walkers out there to come a half of a mile across the open without a weapon if you can manage it!"

That at least made David smile, he knew at that point that since they had agreed upon being covered that they probably weren't bandits, and since they were at least being cordial he would give them the benefit of the doubt. "OK soldier, come on in, we are going to keep you covered, but we need those pistols prior to going inside. Besides, you are packing knives and we can cover you."

Hollywood came across the radio, "Still looks good boss, they will have one on the room coving the northern approach, just got a better look at him." Moon confirmed that the person in the other room was on the north side of the building also. "OK David," said Achilles, "sounds agreeable enough to us, let's do this then."

As they approached, they each got out their Micro-Compact .45's that they were carrying, handed them to David's bigger friend, and followed them inside the gas station. When they got inside, David turned to them and shook their hands, introduced his larger friend as Bear, and then released the shake. Achilles nodded at Bear, then introduced himself. "I am Colonel Achilles, US Army, and this is Major Meat, we are glad to meet you two."

David said, "Come on out of there, Mom," and from behind a sheet covering a door, a 50 odd year old woman emerged holding a double barrel shotgun. "This is Mom, she's my wife, any funny business and she will turn that skater-gun on you guys, do we have an understanding?"

"Sure thing David, no worries," replied Achilles.

David got out a canteen of water and five cups from behind the counter that was probably in the past a cash register station or something like that. The rest of the gas station innards were prepped like a mini version of the Alamo. Sandbags and other things made it a miniature fort. "This is our version of a listening post, gentlemen, if we can come to an agreement and you meet some our demands, we can take you back to the Fort, and maybe even give you a place to refit." That sounded good to the team, but there would have to be negotiations first.

"David," Achilles began, "we are part of a mission that the government started prior to all of this shit happening. We are really in the blind about what is going on, the situation heading to the west, and really are just figuring some things out. We are sworn to protect the Constitution of the United States of America, against all enemies foreign and domestic. We aren't here to hurt anyone, or try to take anything, we can provide you with our Identification Cards, and give you our word that we won't do anything to harm or hurt any of your people, but all I can give you besides that is my word as an Officer and a Gentleman."

"Well Mr. or Colonel," said David, "we haven't seen very many soldier types that were in the correct uniform since about two months after the Reckoning as some have started to call it. We have a little problem since some of the soldiers in the past have turned out to be nothing more than pirates or bandits, or scum. We get some people trying to get into our community every couple of weeks, they come from the west and try to take what isn't theirs. I hope that the two of you can understand, but trust really isn't given these days, it's earned."

"Mr. David, sir, we can understand that, you are the first humans that we have come across in quite a while." A little white lie, they had only been a team for four days, and had only been in this wasteland for a little over 36 hours, but David wouldn't know that, and that was all part of their OPSEC (Operational Security) anyway. "We are just looking for what we said, information, possibly some supplies that we can do our best to work or pay for, and to get on down the road towards our goal."

"That is funny, a goal, haven't heard anyone use that for quite some time, do you care to elaborate on what that goal may be?" David questioned.

Achilles didn't think that it would hurt to maybe share a little, being vague was part of being an elite unit when dealing with the local population. "We are heading west, just like I said earlier, going to Colorado to hopefully link up with our Command, haven't had contact with them in a long time, but we think that they should be there."

This little bit of information seemed to spark some interest in David. "When all the bad things started to happen, we were told on the news and after for a while from the radio broadcasts before they stopped that, that all of the Brass from Washington had headed to some top secret location in Colorado. We all laughed, even had a few radio addresses from the President in the early days, guaranteeing that we would survive the dead, that the wars weren't really wars, and all of that mumbo jumbo."

Achilles and Meat were taking it all in, to be exact the entire team was taking it all in via the radios. To be honest, Achilles was surprised that David hadn't asked about the rest of his team since they were wearing ear pieces and had radios on their backs. Things at least were shaping up to be good with this meeting. David poured them all some water, both soldiers thanked him and waited to see the other two men and Mom take a drink. Kind of funny, but they still had the ability to be nice even though in reality they were shooters. Achilles' own mother said one time that "You and your Army buddies can be on the best behavior of anyone that I have ever met, but let something bad happen and you are ready to kick ass!" That made Achilles stifle a chuckle, his mom always had a way of saying things in a no shit type of way.

As the group of survivors were talking, David started telling them about the Day of Reckoning. He was going into how and why they were had managed to survive, and just a general overview of things, when they were interrupted by a man coming down a ladder. At the same time Achilles was being given the news via earpiece from Hollywood. "Boss, we have contact to the east, looks like about 700 meters, I see two men on motor bikes, a technical vehicle (truck or car with weapons on it), and it looks to be about six people. Correct that, second technical vehicle to the northwest in the field about 900 meters."

The man coming down the ladder turned out to be a teenage boy, ratty beard and wearing a hodgepodge of clothing. "Dad, we have some unfriendlies coming from the city it looks like, Sis says that there are two motorcycles and a truck heading this way!"

"Shit," said David, "raiders, haven't seen or heard them in weeks, this is not what we need right now! OK, Colonel, if you have anyone else with you, now may be a good time and come clean about how many you are, and if you think that you can give us a hand before this turns ugly. We will have these raiders to deal with, and if we survive that, then probably some runners then walkers that they are stirring up with those damn bikes!"

"David, we can help you guys out," said Achilles. "Can my man here get on the roof with one of your rifles? Also, we need those handguns back now!"

"No worries, you guys help us out, we may even just help you re-supply and make this be your payment," said David. With that being said, Meat followed the boy up to the roof, told Woody that he would be coming up top, and to try and keep eyes on the Tangos (Bad Guys) that were heading their way.

"All Seeker elements, this is Achilles, maintain eyes on target, provide support to us and our friends here. Moon, get that Stryker in position so that Ope can man the .50, do not, I say again, do not engage unless you have a confirmed target... break... Hollywood, if they come closer and engage, take em' out, try to disable the vehicles with the Barrett... break... Meat, sit rep? Over." All of these commands that had just flowed out put the team into position, no one needed to ask questions, no one needed to be told what to do, it was just second nature to them.

"Boss, they are inbound, I have a 30.06 here that this young man has handed me, I will keep eyes on, looks like about a minute to contact if they stay inbound, Over," Meat reported in.

David looked to Achilles. "I'm pretty sure these are the so called 'Greencastle Regulars,' they are a bunch of college kids that made it, and have become basically a bunch of bullies that try to take people's stuff for nothing!"

Inside the station Achilles had a great vantage point, high ground, and a fortified position. It would be a great place to stay provided that these thugs had no artillery. "David, do these guys have anything that you know of in the way of explosives?" It was a simple question, and David replied, "Not really, they use random guns, shotguns, and a few rifles, you can bet they have some snipers somewhere out there with them. They only come every few weeks, we stay down and out of the way when they are around. They just kind of probe us, they have taken some hostages in the past, but we have never received any demands to get our people back." This was beginning to play out just like places such as Afghanistan and other shit holes that some of the team members had been to, well-armed thugs who ran amuck when there was no other form of justice to keep them contained. "David," asked Achilles, "how do you want to handle this? It's your show, my men can support you, but we aren't going to stay put here, we have a mission to accomplish and I don't want to bring anything onto you guys." David looked worried, most people who aren't trained become battle hardened when times get tough, some others just shut down when the bullets start to fly. Hopefully David would prove to be the first type.

"OK soldier," replied David, "it's best to see if they just go by us, they may shoot a few times, throw a Molotov cocktail at the building here, and maybe just keep going. If they stop and really try to bring down the rain, then we need to try to kill them! I hate to say that, but they really just seem to be the scum of the earth!"

"Sounds good to us, David, you just give the word, and we will do what you need us to do. I don't want to get any of my men wounded or killed here, so we will play it your way. Say the word and we will put them down." All of this flowed from Achilles like butter, he had said words like this many times over the last few years. It would look to outsiders as if these soldiers were cold and collected, no apprehension, no fear, but to the team, they were all nervous, the kind of nervousness that is bestowed upon men when they fight for their own existence as a way of life, as a soldier who has seen combat in their day.

"Boss, they are 200 meters out, two have dismounted from the truck, the two on bikes are sitting there, one is pointing and giving directions, Over," .... came from Woody.

"We have eyes on them now, let's play this cool and try to avoid this fight if we can, if we shoot from the building, Woody and Moon, take out the vehicles. Dismounts will be easier to handle, Over," Achilles relayed his commands to his team. With that there were four clicks of microphones, that was a standard way of relaying that the message had been received and they understood the orders.

CHAPTER 7
SHOWDOWN AT THE SHELL STATION

The first few minutes of any contact will always set in motion a chain of events and a bit of chaos. Until a side could establish dominance it always went this way. When men with guns have problems, cooler heads never seem to prevail. These words played over and over again in Achilles' head every time that he was forced into a battle. These words had been told to him by an instructor at Ranger School. He always found himself thinking of that whenever the shit was about to hit the proverbial fan.

"Hello in there!" came a voice over a handmade megaphone. "We just want you to turn over your weapons and come with us, there is no need for any shooting, you're trapped and we have the upper hand. I give my word that no one will be hurt, and that we are only doing what is best for you!" David chuckled at this, the last time some of his people had heard that same speech, they were taken away, save for Kit, she had hid in the woods and made it back by the skin of her teeth. She was on the run for two days, avoiding runners and walkers, and trying to evade the captors.

"David," asked Achilles, "what is the plan?"

"Well," David responded, "I think that maybe we could ask them to leave, or maybe you can use that rank you have and try to talk them down, either way, we aren't going with them!"

Achilles mulled it over in his head. Maybe going out and trying to talk some sense into these men could work, they were all younger, but sometimes that youth and the lack of rules made people stubborn. "OK, David, why don't I try to talk to them, maybe see if we can all go our separate ways?" All Achilles got from David was a nod, the man looked scared, this wasn't something that you were prepared for prior to the world going to shit, and that nod told Achilles all he needed to know. "Hey out there, my name is Col. Achilles, United States Army, I will come out and meet your leader half way between you and our position, how does that sound?"

That got the thugs thinking, maybe even a little on edge. Hollywood had them dead to rights in his scope, and he let Achilles know this.

"Colonel. Huh, I wasn't aware that there was a U.S. Army any more, they all took off after the bombs came! What do you think I am out here, stupid?"

"This man sounds like a hard-ass," said Achilles. "Doesn't have any manners either."

He then directed his voice to the men outside. "OK out there, we can go with option two then, get back into your vehicles and head back from where you came, we will not be surrendering!" That actually got the thugs laughing; they thought it was a real knee slapper according to both Meat and Hollywood who were watching them through scopes.

"I think we will go with option one Colonel Sanders, you come on out here and quit being a hero, and we can all go back to our base and sort this thing out!"

With that Moon came across. "Who does this guy think he is? You are in a hardened position on the high ground, he can't be serious!"

"How about option three then?" This came from Achilles. "You turn around now and leave, or we will be forced to open fire and take you into custody!" That seemed to make the thugs mad and get them into action, this is really what Achilles was trying to do, make them overzealous and overconfident.

"We tried to let you down easy in there Col. Numbnuts! You will regret ever talking down to the Regulars! Rot in hell!"

Achilles checked his weapon, looked around and asked if there were any more weapons. David looked at his mom and she came forward and handed her double barrel over to him. Achilles nodded to her; she also handed him eight shells. The motorbikes started up, and the thugs started their attack. As soon as they started in, Hollywood put the farthest one out. He had a direct hit through the man's chest, and blew him right off of the bike. Meat took care of the second rider, splitting his head open like a cantaloupe just 10 yards from the technical vehicle. The rest scurried into the truck and started driving toward the station. A bullet hissed by Meat in the roof. "Contact," he said. "We have someone sniping at us up here. Woody, a little help please!" With that Woody just clicked his mic, sitting and waiting for another shot. Meat heard another whiz bang and kept his head down. The truck was heading straight at the station. Moon opened up with the .50 and scored direct hits to the radiator and the front tires. The truck stopped in place 50 feet from the front door. With that there was the loud report of the Barrett, and the simple response, "sniper down." Meat and the young man and woman on the roof put their sights on the truck. It had lasted a whole 45 seconds.

"OK out there," said Achilles. "We have you covered, you are out manned and out gunned, your vehicles are out of commission. Come out with your hands up and guns on the ground!"

At this point the thugs had no other options, they were beat, and they knew it. Their leader sounded off with a simple "OK." They got out of the truck, placed their weapons on the ground, and walked forward 10 feet. Achilles handed the scatter gun back to Mom. She was smiling and he could tell that this made her happy, there was even a tear running down her check. Achilles wasn't through yet. He came out of the building knowing that Meat and Hollywood were covering him, had his .45 in his hand and started to approach the thugs. "Get on the ground face first, hand behind your backs," is all the he said. They followed his instructions and did as they were told. Achilles spoke into the mic. "Team, rally on the Shell station, get the Stryker up here ASAP, we have some people to interrogate."

While Moon, Woody and Opie were getting the Stryker to the station, Meat and Achilles were flex cuffing (Zip Tying) the thugs. David worried that the walkers and probably some runners would be coming, drawn to the noise of battle, and told the young man from the roof to get the horses. "Horses?" asked Achilles. "Yeah, they don't require fuel and can eat grass and grain, we have an abundance of those items," said David. That seemed to make a lot of sense to the team, they could eat you out of house and home, but rather easy to provide their fuel source. Achilles got the four prisoners to their feet, all looked to be between 20-24 years old. The rest of the team had brought the Stryker up to the station and were keeping an eye on things. David's crew were in shock, here these soldiers were negotiating with them, and even helping them out of a tight spot. They could have used the Stryker vehicle and wiped them off of the planet, but they had been nice and even cordial about their negotiations. This is something that David and his people had not been accustomed to since the world had basically ended.

"David," said Achilles. "What can we do to help you out with these guys? They are yours to deal with, we can do something for you with them, but we need to get back on the road by tomorrow morning. We didn't mean to come in here and stir up the hornets' nest, and I hope we haven't caused you any trouble."

"No worries sir, I never meant any disrespect by calling you soldier boy; we just haven't had anyone act civil in a long time."

"Well David, how do you want to handle this riff raff that we have here?

David thought about it for a moment carefully before framing his reply. "I think we should take them hostage and maybe even try to coordinate a hostage exchange. Of course we will need to blindfold them before heading back to our … place."

Moon came out and told Achilles and the group he had an idea. "Why don't we put them in the Stryker and that way they would not know the way to so called place that David was referring to?"

The team put the prisoners in the Stryker, patted down and zip tied together. There was no way they were getting free. David agreed to let them come back to their place, it was the least he could do since the team had handled the thugs. It was a tight fit in the Stryker, Meat was at the wheel, Moon and Opie inside monitoring the radios and guarding the prisoners, and Hollywood and Achilles riding up top. They moved west of the intersection about a mile and half, that's when they turned onto an old grown over dirt road. If one was to look very closely you could see the hoof marks in the ground from the horses. David, riding next to the Stryker on his horse,, told them to keep their eyes on the woods, sometimes they got some company from the walkers and runners, but since it was around noon it shouldn't be a concern. He went on to explain matter-of-factly, as if it was common knowledge, that you would have to do a lot to get them moving during daylight hours. He said he would bet his left nut that the station would be crawling with them tonight.

After about a 10 minute ride they came out into a clearing. "These people have their shit together," said Meat over the ICS. "They have four guard towers and a huge ditch, fence with razor wire, and a drawbridge." This was pretty amazing to the team, but in retrospect if you were going to survive in the new world, you would have to adapt and overcome. They went through the gate after a short stop, where it appeared that David had to do a little explaining. He circled back around on his horse and told them to park wherever they liked, they had a place for the hostages, and that Achilles' team should follow him.

Meat parked the Stryker facing out, that way they could provide a support by fire position at the gate if anything came up. David told them where to take the hostages, a big red barn in the middle of the compound. Opie and Moon got them out and moving. At that point they were taken by a few men and a woman into the barn. The team gathered and shut down the Stryker. David was speaking to some people near a large house, what appeared to be the main house in the compound. The team milled about the Stryker; Achilles told them to stay alert, and if they moved anywhere to maintain coms. They all knew this, but that is what a good leader did. David and his crew came back and initiated the conversation.

"Colonel Achilles, we are very grateful for the help that you provided to us. We want you to know that you and your men are welcome here. We will have dinner at around 6:00 pm, we are roasting a hog tonight and we just can't begin to thank you for your help out there. Trust is a hard thing to come by these days, you have earned it. If there is anything you need, please don't hesitate to ask us."

Achilles responded by thanking him, telling the people that they were proud to help a group of survivors. "What we would like to do is sit down and go over our route out west with you guys, try to get a little bit of an awareness of what we can expect, and then possibly help you get your people back from these thugs."

"I think we will take you up on that honor, Colonel, we don't know much in the way of interrogating people, but from the looks of your team, y'all may be a little better at it than us." David smiled grimly.

The next few hours flew by as the team members looked over maps with the people from the compound. It tuned out that David and some of his people had been on this land for quite some time. They were an old hippie commune that stayed out of the way of the rest of society. Most people around didn't even know that they were here. When the first sign of the dead walking came about, they were prepared. They raided wherever they could to get supplies, built the fence and then dug the 8 foot ditch that surrounded the place. It wasn't hard, they had a backhoe that they used. It was pretty much a working farm where people of like mindedness had come together. Altogether it was a pretty amazing place. They had a well that provided water, and even had a few garden areas near the fence lines that provided fresh vegetables. The barn was big, the team had yet to go inside, but David told them that they had livestock that helped provide food when the hunting wasn't working out. There were four homes or houses on the compound. David told the group there were plenty of extra beds if they wanted a good night's sleep.

While they were going over what had happened, the team learned that large groups or swarms of the infected moved together. They were usually near larger towns, but sometimes they would roam from place to place seeking the living. Runners on the other hand could be anywhere, they were stronger, faster, and seemed to be more intelligent. Of course this information had been gathered while David and his group were running and keeping their heads down. Most of it the team already knew from the news and intelligence that had been provided by Tinker. The best bit of information they were able to gather was that most people just stopped flying after the bombs. The commune hadn't seen a plane in the air since that day. That sparked something in Hollywood's mind. He could fly a plethora of fixed wing aircraft, as well as his primary rotary wing aircraft. That would be discussed when the team was by themselves, OPSEC would require it, but Hollywood would definitely bring it up tonight. If they could find a fixed wing aircraft, then they could cover more ground, therefore getting to Cheyenne with way less danger. Danger wasn't the problem, none of the men in the team worried about that, but it would delay them and time was ticking by. They really needed to rendezvous with someone from the government.

After a great meal of roasted hog, vegetables, and even sweet tea, the team was feeling great. It had been a good 6 hours and they were relaxed and well fed. They were able to refit their water and fuel thanks to David's people. As they were sitting around David explained that they kept the power going without notice from generators that they had underground. That way there was light and they even had heat in the houses. "No air conditioning," David grinned, "but it does get cold in Indiana." That brought up another excellent point. Achilles turned to David. "Do the undead move in the cold? I mean they aren't alive, but do weather changes have any effect on them?" David nodded and told the team that the undead seemed more active at night. In the daytime they just seemed to stand around unless there was a lot of noise. When it got cold they almost seemed to be nonexistent. He wasn't sure if they migrated or just hunkered down in a sleep-like state, there weren't many researchers in the commune, well there weren't any at all if truth be told.

The shared information was great. Achilles and the team showed David the route that they had taken to get there, the amounts of walkers that they had seen, and safe roads that they had taken. "Speaking of which," said David. "We need to interrogate these guys that we took today. Since you guys are soldiers, and good at your jobs, do you want to handle that for us?" That was a good question. All member of this team had attended the SERE "Survive, Evade, Resist, Escape" course at Camp McCall. This had taught them about survival, and about some of the techniques of interrogating captives. This art had been taken to another level with Moon. While in the NSA he had been part of this on many occasions. Most of the team had also done these things, but the NSA, well that was another matter.

"David," said Achilles, "Sergeant Major Moon here can handle that for you, he and Chief Opie would be glad to handle this." This was a little intriguing, and Moon warned David that no one from the compound should be around. It could be messy to say the least, and possibly a little inhumane.

David agreed, spoke to a young man and told him to take the two members of the team to the barn. Achilles gave them a nod, and they followed the young man to the barn. Inside of the barn was pretty amazing. The floor was concrete, there were pens for animals, and a small armory. A few people milled about inside, but they paid no mind to the soldiers. The young man's name was Steve. He gave them a Reader's Digest version of who he was. He had been a student in Indianapolis, got separated from his family, and eventually had been taken in by David. He was here with his family, his young son Carter, and his wife Kelly. It was his job to hunt for and work on any electronics that they came across on their foraging journeys.

Steven explained that there was a bomb shelter under the barn. It had been built in the 1960's during the Cuban Missile Crisis. Inside of it there was enough room and supplies for fifteen people to live for a year or more. They had used it during the bombing, but since Indy hadn't been hit by nukes there wasn't any need to stay inside of it. The prisoners were inside. And Steven took the members down to them.

CHAPTER 8
INTERROGATION

Moon and Opie entered the shelter with Steven. They told him it would be best to wait outside once they began, and to shut the door. They looked around with him and Steven showed them what was down there. Sporadic tools and water, even a bathroom. The prisoners were seated back to back and flex cuffed to support poles. Moon and Opie thanked him and advised him that it was probably time to leave. Steven gave them a look, but understood that this might not be something that he needed to witness. David had said that he wanted his people back, and that he didn't care what happened to the scum that was in the barn.

Steven left the bunker and closed the door behind him. He told the guys to use the intercom on the door when they wanted out. Moon and Opie started by selecting one of the men seated closest to them. Opie went over and got him up, walked him around in circles, sat him down, stood him up, and repeated this process. He wasn't bad to the guy, but the hostage was being pushed around. This was a technique used time and time again throughout history. Confuse the hostage and then interrogate them. Since they were all gagged and had hoods on, they really couldn't do much but hear what was going on. Moon was in a backroom. He had a chair set up, there was a bucket of water, and some needle nose pliers. He had placed his two sidearms and M-4 on a table. His two knives were also set down. He had taken his ACU blouse off and put his gloves on.

Opie then brought the first person in. They had placed marks on the arms of each soldier when they took them captive. Three had black marks on their arms, and one had red. Red was for the leader, he would be the third one to be interrogated. Hostage number one came in, Opie sat him down, then attached an extra zip tie to the chair. He nodded to Moon, closed the door and leaned against it. Moon walked up to the hostage and removed his hood and gag. The young man looked terrified. Moon started by saying, "Hi there, my name is Command Sergeant Major Moon. I am a member of the United States Army. I am also a member of the NSA, do you know what the NSA is, young man? I will elaborate for you. Chief Opie, can you get this young man a drink of water?" With that, Opie got a cup of water and helped the young man drink it. Moon continued. "I will explain, I was a career Army soldier in Special Forces. I joined the NSA or should I say was recruited by them because of my unique skill set. I like to blow stuff up, and also have no problem torturing people." Moon went on to enlighten the young man how the NSA (National Security Agency) had no boundaries. No one questioned what they did, their techniques, or what happened to their detainees.

The young man looked scared to death, Moon hadn't even asked him any questions yet. This always was a good sign to an interrogator. In the Army you are trained to use passive aggression, to tell them enough to keep from getting the shit kicked out of you, but nothing that would compromised your mission or your unit. None of these detainees had any of that training, therefore it would probably be pretty easy. Moon started with a few questions to put the young man at ease.

"What's your name?"

"K-Kyle…" the young man stuttered nervously.

"How old are you?"

"21."

"Where are you from?"

"Acton, Indiana."

"What was your major?"

"Economics. What…what are you going to do to me?"

Moon ignored him. "Do you have any family?"

"No clue, haven't been very far from here since the bombs."

"Do you enjoy taking from others?"

"No sir… I just follow orders from the guys at the Frat House, we are just trying to stay alive."

"How many people have you killed?"

"None, I promise, no one, I swear!" Kyle started blubbering.

"Are you scared?"

"Yes sir, I don't want to die!"

Moon said, "That's good. Provided that you answer all of my questions, cooperate, and then these people agree, we will let you live, but if you lie to me, well then this can go very badly for you, do you understand?"

"Yes sir!" Kyle looked slightly relieved at Moon's promise.

"Where is your base located at?"

"At DePauw University."

"Tell me about your base."

"It's our Fraternity house, we have it secured. I stayed when I figured out that it wasn't safe to head home. I just want to go home!" Kyle started to tear up again. He was very young but Moon steeled his heart against any sympathy. That was also part of his training.

"How many men do you have at your base?"

"Twenty-three, there are twenty-three of us."

"Why have you taken hostages?"

"We only took the two girls, we are treating them well, they were students at DePauw, they really aren't prisoners, we just brought them back to the Frat house. The one is Jason's ex-girlfriend. She was from here in town, she is some guy named David … David's daughter. Jason was frantic to get her back. We haven't hurt them, I swear it."

"You know what Kyle, I believe you. Have some water, then we are going to put your gag back on, question your friends, and then we will see what David and Col. Achilles want to do with you. Can you do me a favor?"

"Yes sir, just don't hurt me."

"OK, that's good, Kyle, I am going to put you back out there, no hood. If I don't get what I want out of your leader, I will shoot you!"

Kyle's eyes went wide with fear

Moon smiled grimly at him. "Let me rephrase that, I will act as if I am shooting you. That way maybe I can get him to cooperate. As long as I get cooperation from your buddies, and can collaborate your story, you will not be hurt, do you understand me?" With that Kyle nodded his head, acknowledging his agreement.

Ope and Moon repeated this process two more times; they had decided to hold off and interrogate the leader until after the rest of them. They even made one of them take a few slaps and told him to cry out. They never really touched him, all open handed and the young man went along with it. They found out that all three were scared, didn't like the way that Jason was handling their lives, and the fact that he had taken so much control over them. The young men were all in over their heads. None of them wanted to die, they were just a bunch of college kids that were trying to stay alive. Actually Moon and Opie understood the fact that maybe they were trying to survive, they just didn't agree with their tactics.

James was brought in last, this would be the longest interrogation. After he was shuffled around and brought in, Opie left the room and had food brought to the other captives. This showed them that they cared about them, and would hopefully cause them to turn on Jason. Moon just kept him in the chair and observed him. Jason was squirming around, trying to listen. He looked and acted like he was scared, but was also trying to put on a good show.

Ope came back in and slammed the door. He and Moon got into position, and ripped the hood off of Jason. Opie had his Streamlight LED pointed straight in his face, and Moon threw a bucket of water into it. This would be more shock and awe than the others had faced. Moon then started in with the question.

"What's your name?"

"Jason," he relied sullenly.

"What is your serial number?"

This perplexed him. "Serial number, what are you talking about?"

"Serial number!"

"I don't have a serial number!"

"All soldiers have a serial number, young man, what is yours?"

"I don't have a serial number, I am not a soldier!"

"Well, you may not have one, but since you fired on members of the United States Army while inside of our borders, then you are a terrorist!"

"Whoa, whoa, whoa, I am not a terrorist!" Now Jason did not just look scared, he looked terrified.

"You're not a terrorist huh? Why did you fire on a member of the United States Armed Forces?"

"I was just protecting my men, trying to get food, that is all!" Jason shouted defiantly.

Opie backhanded him, knocking him out of his chair. All of this was part of the technique, wear down the adversary and get what you need from them. The young man was looking scared to death, he wasn't trained for this, and they knew it. Wearing him down wouldn't be all that hard. They just went through the motions like they were dealing with any other prisoner. They left the room, and went back into the main area where the other prisoners were. After a few mikes, they went back into the room. And they started it all again.

"What's your name?"

"Jason. But you know this. What are you..."

Opie slapped him, then Moon casually went on with his questioning. "Are you a terrorist?"

"No, no sir, I am not a terrorist, just a student trying to stay alive."

"Why did you attack members of the United States Military?"

"I, uh, we haven't seen anyone from the military for a long time, we didn't believe it. I am sorry, it was stupid, it's a no man's land out there, we try to take what we need so that we can survive! That's all, I swear it!"

"Why did you take the girls?"

"Who, Julie? She is my girlfriend, she is happy with me!"

"Your men tell me different, they say you took her against her will, are you lying?" "No... she wanted to come with us, she hasn't asked to come back!"

"How many are in your so called 'Regulars?'"

"We had twenty-three till you guys killed two of them!" Jason sneered at Moon.

"You attacked, you were asked to leave, why didn't you leave?"

"We just were trying to get supplies, that station has things we could use!"

"I have one more question for you, young man, and before you answer, you better think about it. The way that you answer this could guarantee your safety and that of your men, and if you answer wrong, I will execute one of them! Do you understand me?"

"Yes, sir, (gulp) yes, sir, I do understand you."

"Where is your base, and will you surrender you and your men to David's authority?"

With that Jason spit on the floor, a little bit of blood from Opie's last backhand slap dribbling from his lip. "NO! I will never do what that old hippie tells me to do!"

Moon jerked him up, grabbed the silenced .45 and pushed him out the door, making an effort to rattle him around a little. He made sure that he was looking at the men, holding him by the neck, and told Opie to do it. With that Opie shot one of the prisoners, well at least it looked like he shot him, the young man doubled over just like he had been told to do. Jason started to weep. Moon then shoved him back into the room, and Jason hit the floor in the corner and openly cried.

Moon and Opie gathered their things, left Jason bound in the room, secured the door and went back into the main room. They explained things to the three that had agreed to cooperate, and then told topside that they were ready to come out. They escorted them up and out of the barn. Outside Achilles and David were waiting on them. All three young men apologized and told them they would do whatever David requested. They just wanted to be safe, and to provide safety and a better living for their fraternity brothers. The next few minutes flew by. They told everything to David and Achilles, numbers, weapons, supplies, and the fact that most of the brothers had begged Jason to link up with the other group for months. Strength in numbers was the smart thing to do, but Jason was stubborn. He had been Captain of the football team, and was very controlling of everything. That was a tricky thing, taking someone in command and putting them under someone else's authority. The young man had done well in keeping his people alive in these days and times of uncertainty.

Darkness was approaching, this was when things would get interesting according to David. There were bound to be numerous undead in the area after the activities of the day. He explained that they generally would come near the compound, and after the sun came up and they were more passive that they would put them down as quietly as possible. After a little more conversation, the three young men convinced David that they and the rest of the brothers would be more than cooperative in coming to the compound. That they all would come in and swear allegiance, and that they were all just scared in the past by the way that Jason had acted. Moon spoke to Achilles and David about what to do with Jason. "Is he scared now?" asked Achilles. Opie actually laughed and told the group that he was probably shitting himself after thinking he had seen one of his own executed.

Achilles, David, Opie and Moon all went back to the bomb shelter. They went inside and found Jason laying with his back against the wall and looking like he had just lost his puppy. The rest of the interrogation went like this.

"Young man, I am Col. Achilles, United States Army, I am going to ask you some questions. If I don't like what you have to say, my large friend over here will beat the shit out of you, do you understand?"

"Yes sir."

"Do you know that I am sworn to protect the Constitution of the United States against all enemies, foreign and domestic? That I am sworn to obey the orders of the President of the United States and the officers appointed to me? That it is my job in times of chaos to bring law and order to this nation? That I also have no need to keep you alive?"

" ...Yeah, ye...yes sir."

"OK then, we have an offer for you. Since you have provided safety to your brothers, and proved to be rather crafty, don't you think that coming into this community would be smart, that teaming up and providing strength in numbers would provide a better sanctuary for your people?"

"…Yes sir, it's just that, that, that man David hates me, I just want to marry his daughter and keep her safe!"

"David has agreed to let you people come here, that you can be one of his people, that he trusts you and as long as you can help to provide, that you will be an asset to this community, is that agreeable to you?"

"It is, as long as we can be together and you won't execute any more of my men, I will take the offer, please, please let us stay here!"

"OK then, we will need to coordinate getting the rest of your men here, I have your word you will obey David's orders. I have appointed him Sheriff of this part of Indiana, I have the authority to do so, and if you disobey him, he can do what is necessary, do you understand?"

"… Yes sir, you have my word." Jason looked defeated.

They escorted him topside to see his men. He was so relieved that they were all there and not dead, he cried and thanked the team; he was overjoyed to find his men all safe and eating. This showed Achilles and the team members that they had done the right thing.

The last bit of sunlight was spent gathering David and the new members in the kitchen at the large house. David and Jason actually worked well together, it was for certain that they knew one another, and looked as if David may have already had considered this young man to be his future son-in-law, no matter what had transpired in the past. The group formed a plan, they would take the Stryker and Jason onto campus, get his men together, and get them all back to the compound. The plan was formed, and David showed everyone to places to settle in. They would retrieve the rest of his element around 1100 hours the next day, that way there would be less activity from the undead. David posted guards, and told the team that they were safe from the outside.

Achilles and the men decided that sleeping near the Stryker was best for their own security. They should provide their own security via the scopes in the vehicle, and the fact that they could be readily available in case of a breach of security. Night fell upon them and they started out their sleeping patterns and guard duties. This was the first night that they would be sleeping outside of the Stryker. The team had slept on different continents and in different situations while doing their former jobs in the military. Woody chose to sleep inside, joking that aviators slept in hotels while in the field. Moon, Meat, Woody, Opie, then Achilles was the order of guard duty. David told them that they had their towers manned, and if there was a breach they would be alerted. Achilles settled in, and tried to get some shut eye.

CHAPTER 9
NIGHTTIME AND DELTA CHI

Around 0100 hours came the first moans and wails of the undead. All member of the team except for Hollywood were up and looking out through their night vision. Being inside, he didn't hear the wails and moans. David had come out of his house and was standing talking to Achilles. "Colonel. You never really get used to it, do ya?" he asked. Achilles was vague but explained the whole undead thing was rather new to them. He explained that he couldn't elaborate, but they had been on a mission, and they were rather new to this new world. They chatted a bit longer. David explained that he had been in Vietnam with the 25th Infantry Division. He spoke about tunnels and being sent in with a flashlight and a .45. "I know that there are missions that the government does, things that common folk have no idea about." He went on to say he was sorry about the way that they first met. He thanked Achilles for what they had done, and was rather optimistic about bringing the fraternity boys into the fold. He explained that Jason was from a rich family in Indianapolis, that he and his daughter were quite in love, and that as a father he had discouraged the relationship, something about thinking no one was good enough for their daughters. He chuckled.

That was the first real time that Achilles thought about his own family. His mom and dad, his brother and sister, and the daughter that he had that lived with them. His dad was crafty, and a survivor. He had served two tours in Vietnam before getting out and working for the CIA. He had a house on Tybee Island, and Achilles hoped that his father and family were OK. Thoughts like that had to be kept deep, he knew this, and hoped that someday he would find them.

David explained that the loud wails were from runners, they would come first, and just stay outside of the ditch and wail and try to find a way in. Then the moans came from the walkers. They would blindly come toward the light, stumble into the ditch, and just mill about until morning when David and his team would put them down. "Head shots, that's what kills them. If you hit them and don't sever the spinal cord, they just get back up. We burn them then. They have to be dead, I mean very dead. If they bite you, scratch you, or you ingest their blood, you are a goner. We burn them in the ditch, that way we don't have to pick them up. The runners have to be thrown in, we put on gloves, masks, and other items to keep the blood off of us. We then wash down with bleach and try to sterilize ourselves." Achilles took it all in. Great information that just helped with what they had learned in the Hangar.

Daytime came. There were around thirty-five walkers that had stumbled into the ditch, just milling about and moaning at the people in the towers. There were seven walkers, all walking about trying to figure out a way across the ditch. David's men came out with a sprayer and put gas on the walkers, then they were set on fire. The stench was terrible, but it had to be done. Achilles and the team took care of the runners, they put them down with head shots from the suppressed .45's. They were all gathered, put in the ditch and set on fire.

David was very helpful, he even provided an old Military 2-1/2 ton truck, known as a deuce and a half. The Commune had bought it at an auction, and it was in good shape. That way they could get the fraternity members in one vehicle. Jason was very helpful to say the least. He told Achilles and the team about their weapons, he was a little vague about where they came from, but for the most part he and David were working great together. Jason would ride in the deuce with Moon at the wheel. Hollywood would man the gunner's turret of the Stryker, and Meat would drive it. Achilles decided that he and Opie would ride in the back of the deuce to handle any walker or runners that they came across. The route would be simple, back to the station and down the road that led to Greencastle and Campus. They would make the run and have a half mile straight shot to the fraternity house. When they got there, Jason and Achilles would gather the survivors and a few things that they could carry, and get back in the truck. They would exfill along the same route that they came, with the exception of getting back to the main road. They would take the street south of them, and hit the main road.

Jason told Achilles that they had put down hundreds of walkers, and most of the campus was rather free of the infected. They had occasional groups, and a few runners, but they did their best to get rid of them in the last few months.

It was a simple plan, but like all plans Achilles and the team would be ready for fragos (Fragmentation Orders, or changes in plans) that they would have to deal with. The team mounted up, everyone had their com checks and weapons checks completed. Before they left David came up to Jason. "I know we have had our differences, son, but you and your people are welcome here. Whatever you and my daughter decide, I will support." That looked to bestow a little bit of confidence in the young man. It wasn't that he wasn't a good kid, it's just that David was not one for ritz, glamour, and rich people. In retrospect no one was rich anymore, at least rich in the way with money. You could only be rich in life these days.

The two vehicle convoy got on the road. They made good time as they turned north toward campus. Jason let them know that it was only a few miles, and the road was clear. They used it every day on their supply runs, and in the heat of the day most of the zombies would be in the hazy state of mind. Moon looked over at him and handed him a pistol. It was his backup and he thought that the young man should be armed. "Here ya go, don't make me regret this!" Jason nodded and thanked him. He advised Moon that the turn would be in a half of a mile, and Moon relayed the info to the rest of the team.

As they approached the turn Hollywood let the team know that there were a few walkers up ahead just staring at nothing. Achilles told him that they would take care of them if they moved. As the convoy rounded the corner the walkers started to move toward the noise. Their guttural moans were drowned out by the engines. Achilles and Opie put them down with aimed precision.

"Ninth house on the left," Moon relayed from Jason to Meat. They came to a stop, Hollywood kept the west covered and Opie would stay in the truck and cover the East. Meat jumped out and took the north avenue of approach. Moon dismounted and took the south. Achilles spoke over the radio to the team. "If anything comes, put them down fast, let's get this done so we can get back on our way ASAP."

The front door opened and Jason yelled to the sentry to get everyone up and gathered and to get a move on it. There was no apprehension from the guard, he followed what Jason had told him and went back inside the structure. Jason and Achilles followed him inside. The lower floor was a marvel to Achilles: a classic fraternity house turned into a fortress. Windows and doors were boarded and reinforced with rebar. They had actually made it into one hell of a castle was all that Achilles could say. It took about 5 mikes, but all the member came inside the main room. Most were kids, 20 to 22 years old, and the two girls were with them. There were a few older guys, 25-27 years in age, but in college there were always older guys. They were either the guys who never wanted to leave college, or possibly ex-military back in school to get a degree. Achilles kept this in the back of his head for when they were back at the commune.

All the gathered looked tired and like they had been through a lot. Jason started to explain. "Brothers, this is Colonel Mountjoy from the U.S. Army, his men and I have decided it's best to relocate to the commune. I know we haven't gotten along with them, but things have changed, we need to move, and we need to move now." There were questions, people looking bewildered at the changes, and what looked like was the beginning of a debate.

Achilles stepped forward. "Gentlemen, ladies, we can have this conversation when we get back, anyone that doesn't want to stay there is free to leave, get your gear and get into the truck. This is not a debate, and not a democracy, you have two minutes to get your stuff, then we are moving out!" That seemed to get people going; they were 'moving and shaking' was the best way to describe it. A few guys came down carrying guns, everything from pistols to shotguns, to rifles. They would have to help if things went wrong.

Achilles stepped out, saw that Moon and Opie were firing to the south. "Any problems?" he said over the radio. "Nothing big, just a few walkers coming down the alley, we are dealing with them," replied Moon. "All clear," came from Hollywood and Meat.

The group had reassembled when Achilles stepped back in, he told them to run straight to the truck, and get in as fast and safely as possible. No one disobeyed the order, Jason and Achilles were the last out, and Jason secured the door. They helped the rest board the truck, and Achilles signaled to the team it was time to bug out. With that they turned south two blocks and got moving back toward the main road. They were moving at about 30 miles per hour when Moon told Achilles it looked like runners up ahead. And runners is what they were.

Three of them were running toward the street. Achilles told Woody to put them down, and he opened up with the .50 cal. If it wasn't such a sweet sight to see them torn to shreds, it would have been disgusting. They had no chance, but Achilles and the rest of the team noticed that they even tried to dodge the shots, it seemed that the noise brought them out of the dream-like state that most of them were in. The convoy made the turn and headed back down the road to the station. The rest of the way back was clear, they didn't see any more undead and made it to the compound unscathed. From start to stop, the mission was a success in under an hour, much quicker than the team could have anticipated. They would count this up as lucky, and hope that the rest of the journey west would be the same.

The makeshift drawbridge was raised, and the team and all of the new inhabitants of the commune dismounted. There were cheers and a happy set of hugs and kisses from David's family and their daughter. The other girl reunited with her family also. Achilles didn't know them, but got a nod from the father as thanks.

David, Jason and the rest of the community (except for those in the guard towers) gathered at the Barn. David's speech was inspiring, and made Achilles feel good about the way that things looked to be shaping up. David started, "Brothers and Sisters, we have a great thing here. Thanks to Col. Achilles and his men, we have reunited two families, and brought a great number of men into this compound to make our numbers greater. Jason and his men are good at scrounging equipment and supplies and we should be a good bit safer. Jason has agreed to follow what we decide, but also will be my second in command. With us working together we should be safer and stronger in the future!" That got a number of claps and hoots and hollers from everyone gathered. At that point David stepped forward. "Col. Achilles," he began, "we are going to solidify our association with the brothers here. My daughter has decided, and I have blessed her marrying Jason. We would be honored if you would perform the ceremony for us, to be honest there is no preacher, and if this were a ship, the Captain could do this for us." That took Achilles by surprise. The team seemed to laugh about it, but it all made sense.

"David, when would we be doing this?" Achilles asked with a smile.

"Well, we thought about tonight, I know that you plan on getting on with your mission in the morning, so we thought we could do it now." And with that, there was nothing that Achilles could do but accept the invitation.

At 1900hrs Col. Achilles and his men were outside near a bon fire and speaking to Jason. He had two of his men with him; they would serve as groomsmen. Achilles had learned that his bride to be was named Susan. Her maid of honor was Kit, and they would come out when they were ready. The members of the community had gathered on hay bales and chairs on the bride's side. The brothers of Delta Chi were on the side of the groom. The father and the bride came out and down the stairs, they even had a guy playing the guitar and strumming "Here Comes the Bride." David brought his daughter up the aisle, followed by Kit, the maid of honor. He kissed his daughter, and handed her off after a handshake from Jason.

Achilles did his best to make the ceremony seem official. He talked about the love a man and a woman share for one another, the sanctity of marriage, and the role a husband and wife play to one another. It was simple and to the point. Jason gave her his high school class ring, and it was as official as possible. The ceremony was followed by food and wine that they had brought up from the shelter. It was a good evening, and everyone came by and thanked the members of the team for what they had done. This could be one of the best things for all the members of the fraternity and the commune. Achilles hoped it proved to be a blessing and not a calamity. He spoke with David, assured him that if they got into contact with the government that they would be made aware of the fact that there were still survivors here, and that they needed help.

The team had some food, even a glass or two of the wine. It made them laugh, but for the first time in a long time they smelled marijuana. It was a bunch of hippies and college students, and there was not really any law against it now. They laughed and joked that they could probably get high and no one would say anything about it.

Hollywood then turned to ask Achilles if he was open to a new suggestion about how they were to head west. Achilles started by telling the team that he was open to any suggestion, this was a team, but they needed to all try to figure things out, and not to be worried about voicing an opinion. "You are all soldiers, I appreciate the fact that you have suggestions, and I value each and all of your input. Please never think that I don't, I am just as lost as all of you out here."

Hollywood stated that he and Moon had been checking out the route. Terre Haute would be the next town they would come across, or at least the first town of any significance. Although at Atterbury they were limited to what types of aircraft there were, but Hullman Regional outside of town might have better options. They could scout it out, and there might be a plane that they could requisition. It would really speed up their journey, and High Frequency radios might even be able to put them in contact with any remnants of the government. It was a great idea, Moon said he and Opie knew the area, he had dated a girl that went to school in Terre Haute when he was first out of high school and before the Army. The idea of flying was great, they could try to get all of the airfields all the way to Cheyenne Mountain mapped out, and even possibly get fuel. Hollywood went on to say that they could use the Stryker to try and get the battery on a plane charged, he had his Airframe and Powerplant License and was a maintenance test pilot on Uh-60 and AH-1H helicopters.

Achilles took it all in, this team really did have their shit together, they were working great as a cohesive unit, and when they had to perform the gelled like they had been together for years. It seemed like a good time for a group meeting, maybe even feel out if they all wanted to continue with the mission. They could reach Cheyenne Mountain and no one could be there, they could possibly find some part of the government, or they could try to eke out an existence and do what was best for themselves. It had had been a hell of quick few days to say the least. But it was time to find out what they would do. Whatever the decision, Achilles would keep heading toward Cheyenne, and he figured everyone else would also.

Achilles called the Pow Wow. They met up inside the barn and used a table that wasn't being occupied by partiers. The atmosphere was relaxing, and just by being there the team could tell that everyone around here needed to let go a little. Moon had brought the maps and a PAD, and Meat had scrounged up a few ice cold Bud's. They tasted like shit and were skunky, but it was better than some other beer that most of them had sampled while in different parts of the world.

The team had started talking when one of the older brothers came up to talk to Achilles. "Sir, my name is Technical Sergeant Basse, I am a member of the Air National Guard here in Indiana. I never got recalled when it happened, and feel like I have betrayed my country in not trying to get back to my unit. I am here to turn myself in." The entire team looked at each other, and Achilles told Moon as the ranking non-commissioned officer to dress this young man down, and then to see if he could handle being part of the team. Moon suggested that he might have some of the skills necessary to help the mission, and they could order him to do so if need be.

"Look here young man," Moon said, "get at Parade Rest when I am talking to you. I am Command Sergeant Major Moon, what was your specialty in the Air Force?"

"I... I... I was a crew chief on cargo planes, Sergeant Major!" Basse stammered.

"Good, why don't you come over here and have a seat, Colonel Achilles would like to have a few words with you."

Achilles asked him about Hullman Field, what kind of planes flew in and out of there. He also asked about the Air National Guard base, about the buildings, aircraft, personnel and everything he could think of. The young man told him everything, drew up a sketch of the hangers, told him what was in the buildings, where the officers were at, and even the Arms Room. This under normal circumstances was a breach of security, even if they were in the military, but these were no longer normal times.

"Sir," said the Sergeant, "I just would like to help our country. I stayed here because I had nowhere else to go, it was the safest thing to do, and if I was wrong for doing that, I will accept any punishment that you are willing to give me."

Achilles just had one question for him, "Sergeant Basse, do you still want to serve your country? Do you want to come with us to try to link up with whoever is in charge?"

"Sir, yes sir! I would love to come with you, I don't have much of my gear, but I will do whatever you guys tell me to do!"

"Have you spoken with Jason and David? I would love to take you with us, your knowledge of Aircraft mechanics would be huge for our mission, do you need me to do that for you?"

"No sir, Jason knew when I saw you that this is what I would do, we have spoken already. He says that it's a free world, do what makes you happy."

"It's settled then, from now on you are part of the team, or at least until someone who outranks me tells me otherwise."

With that being settled the team got to work on a plan, it was simple really, get to the airfield, try to find something with decent range, roomy enough for all of them, and safe enough to get them to Cheyenne Mountain. They spent the next two hours planning flight points, trying to avoid larger airfields that could have great numbers of undead, looking for places close enough to find fuel, and the general route they would take. Achilles told the team to get some shut eye, to sleep close enough to the Stryker that they could be found in case of problems, and gave them the rotation of guard duty.

The team was up, loaded and ready to move out at 0600 hrs. There were larger number of undead at the fences, at least twice as many as the day before. The team shot the runners and some walkers with the suppressed .45's. Then it was time to go. Mom had brought some fresh canned vegetables for them to take with them. "All those MRE's will bind you boys up quicker than a hornet stings you," she said, gave them hugs, and thanked them for all that they had done to reunite her family. David and Jason and a few others came and said their goodbyes. Jason was tearing up a little while talking to Basse, he gave him a M-16A2 and a Beretta 9mm and ammunition that they had pooled together from the brothers' stock of firepower and ammo. David was gracious and apologized once again for the start of their association. Achilles told him not to worry about it, guaranteed that if they were able to find the government, they would let them know about the community. He wished them all well and then the team loaded up the Stryker.

The team headed west via the National Road I-40. It made sense to head this way, it was the most direct route to the airfield. Airfields were great places to hole up in case the situation around Terre Haute was a bad one. You had a perimeter fence, high structures that could afford sanctuary, and buildings that could be secured. The main issue would be the undead in the area, and the team's ability to get in, establish linear danger areas, and avenues of approach while trying to secure an aircraft. It also was a logical choice, and a good place to leave the Stryker. In the wrong hands, this vehicle could rain havoc on a town or community.

Basse looked a bit apprehensive while they were riding out. Achilles could see it on his face, he wasn't necessarily a Special Operations soldier, and probably not too great with a weapon. The team could make him better. Special Forces soldiers specialized in helping to create local forces to handle problems. If anyone in this wasteland could help him learn, it was this team. Achilles would keep him with Opie, and that way he could cover him and also keep the young man's wits about him. Achilles had briefed the team about the mission, and to be vague with Basse about the Top-secret materiel. The young man didn't need to know that, and probably wouldn't even begin to believe them. His story was the usual. Served a few years in the Air Force, got out, stayed in the Air Guard for college money, and was just trying to go through life when the world turned to shit.

The ride should take around an hour. They weren't in a hurry, so Meat kept it around 35 mph. Moon brought up a point that they could all hear over the ICS. He said that they would need to give Basse a call sign, and told him about the way the unit worked. Achilles pondered letting him pick his own call sign, the rest of the unit had done the same, but usually in the Special Operations community, as new members joined teams, the names just came up, and that is what they were called from that point forward. "How do you feel about the call sign 'College Boy?' he asked Basse with a smile in his voice.

Basse chuckled and said that worked for him. The rest of the team got a good laugh out of it, and then got back down to business. Achilles asked the young man, "How much flight time do you have?"

"I have about 3000 hours, mostly as a crew chief and about a 5th as a load master in training."

"Not what I meant, how much stick time do you have?" Achilles clarified.

"Oh, around 300 hours in and out of the simulator, and probably about 100 flying while on long trips," College Boy stated.

Hollywood had informed Achilles that most pilots, well at least good pilots that trusted their crew, generally let them fly a little. It was widely frowned on by commanders and those in charge, but just about every crew chief worth a lick that was part of a flight crew had at one time or another learned how to fly.

"Sir, I also have my private pilot's license. I am not instrument rated or anything like that, but I have 500 hours in single engine and have about 30 in dual engine aircraft," College Boy volunteered.

That little tidbit of information would be huge. Now that the team knew he could work on planes and possibly help Hollywood in a cockpit, it made this young man's stock value increase by two-fold. The continued their talk with him, everyone was loose on ICS, they were all talking and using call signs. Achilles wasn't too sure if he felt left out because of this, but it didn't seem to mind too much to him. After College Boy addressed them as "Sir" a couple of times, they all told him to use the call signs and not worry about using rank. It was no big deal, just to follow the orders that the rest of the team would give to him.

Moving down I40, they saw numerous undead in fields and alongside the road. The team decided that they would keep moving and cut down the ones close to the road with suppressed shots. They would get walkers and runners that would follow the noise indefinitely, but would have to deal with those as the time came. It took about 50 minutes to get within a half mile of the facility.

Everyone in the team dismounted and got eyes on the objective using binoculars and the spotter scope. College Boy told them all the layout, they could see the main gate on the National Guard side. No one was there, the only thing that they saw were a few undead milling about out on the runway, but overall it looked pretty peaceful. That came to no surprise to anyone on the team. Airfields were rather secure, and short of these undead figuring out how to use key codes if there was even power, or having enough of them to storm the fence, there was no way that they could take over the entire airfield.

After about an hour of observation, they formulated a plan. College Boy had told them where the main hangar and all of the aircraft keys were located at the Armory, and the civilian place that had aircraft that people could rent. There looked to be two C-130's, an Army Sherpa, and a fighter jet or two. The other side, or the far side near the main terminal looked to have a few Cessnas and possibly a bigger plane or two in the hangar. The plan was to get to the armory gate, get in, res-secure the gate, and clear the main National Guard Hangar. College Boy even had a key to get in. The only thing that was joked about was "not getting to blow anything up," by Moon. Opie called him a firebug and they all laughed a little.

College Boy, Opie and Moon would get into the hanger, find the keys to the Sherpa or C-130's, and get back to the door. Meat and Achilles would clear as much of the hangar as possible. Hollywood would man the cannon on the Stryker and keep an eye out for unwanted guests. Not too hard of a plan, if there would be contact, they all knew that things would change in a heartbeat. They did a final weapons and commo check, loaded up and motored toward the gate.

The final way took under 30 seconds, Meat was screaming toward the gate. They pulled up and Achilles, Moon, and Opie dismounted. Hollywood said "Shit!" over the mic. "Contact, looks like a gate guard in there is moving, doesn't seem to be able to work the door, he is just pounding on the glass, watch your asses." The three man element went up to the guard building. There was in fact one guard in there that had been exposed, and another that looked like he had been eaten alive. Achilles told them to get the gate open and he would take care of the undead.

Moon and Opie went to work. The gate was secured, but was able to be pushed open with a little bit of resistance since the power was out. Achilles stepped up to the door, looked and observed the former Airman for a few seconds, placed his pistol up to the glass and waited for it come closer. It was rabid like a dog, moaning in a guttural way that would make the skin crawl on most men. It just walked up and kept walking into the door. Achilles lined up, squeezed the trigger, and it dropped. With that the team went through the gate and secured the fence once again, this time using a chain and tent stake that they had in the Stryker's tool kit.

The 200 meters that it took to get to the hangar and the door took a few seconds to cover. The Stryker was pulled up in front, and Hollywood scanned the airfield. If any walkers made it this way, they were to be put down quietly, and everyone knew the drill. The hangar wasn't that large, but with no power it would be dangerous. They would use NVS (Night Vision Devices) to clear the way, and help College Boy find the keys. Opie and Moon would move with him, Achilles and Meat would secure the door and inside of the perimeter of the building.

Inside of the hangar was dark, but it was rather clean. It looked as if no one had been here in quite some time, but there were footprints in the dust. That made them assume that they weren't alone, and there was probably a few walkers on the prowl. The light that came in when they opened the door would alert anything inside to their presence, so they were all a little on edge.

Moon's team walked the fire lane that would lead them to most direct route to the Flight Operations office where the keys were stored. As a crew chief, and as a soldier that had to pull duty, College Boy would be able to access the safe. Achilles and Meat would work forward and clear the main hangar. Moon's team moved toward the office area of the building. They heard shuffling from the front of the hangar, then a few suppressed shots, and the low voice in their earpieces of "Tango Down." They got to the door and Moon and Opie pushed it open. The room was clear. Opie secured the door and College Boy went to work on the safe. Moon told him to do it as quickly as possible, not to be scared, and they would be out of here as quick as he could procure the keys.

Outside in the hangar Meat and Achilles had put down two former members of the Air Guard that looked to have been in here since the beginning. They scouted and cleared the entire inside of the hangar; only two undead were all that they had found. They found a rollaway toolbox, and pushed it toward the door. That could come in handy, at least Woody and College Boy could come up with what they needed out of it.

"Moon, do you copy?" Achilles murmured.

"Copy, we are trying to get into the safe, all clear in here, Over."

"Roger, interior of the main hangar is clear, two walkers put down, Over."

"Roger, stand by."

It took College Boy a few minutes to work the safe, his hands were sweating and it had been a long time since he had to access it. Luckily for the team the combination had not been changed. Inside were keys to five airplanes, an American Flag, and a note.

They exfilled the building, pushed out the toolbox, and secured the door. Woody had dealt with three walkers as they came across the airfield. There appeared to be five or six more, all probably baggage handlers and such that had worked inside of the secure area. The team took the time to take stock on what they had found. Woody and College Boy knew that they always topped off the fuel when a plane landed at the completion of a mission. That shouldn't be a problem. The only problem was the quality of the fuel that had sat inside of the tanks for over a year at least. College Boy told them that they could get some treatment from inside of the hangar if they had to, and that they would just have to get one of the planes APU's "Auxiliary Power Unit" operational so that they could check it over. Pre-flight would be conducted, and the best option would be the one that they would take. Woody suggested the Sherpa C-23. The aircraft was a box with wheels and engines. It wasn't fast, but could take off and land on small strips, had great range, and was relatively easy to fly. They had proved to be worth their weight in gold in Iraq, they were easy to maintain, and not all that sophisticated. The team would be sacrificing firepower and the ability to drive rather than walk. It was a calculated risk, but seemed to be the fastest way to get from point A to B in the least amount of time. They could get all their gear into the craft which was another bonus for the team.

Woody and College Boy went to work. They got into the aircraft, and of course the battery was dead. That would be the first step. College Boy got it out, and took it to the Stryker to try to figure out how to charge it. With a little help from Moon, they got a spark and were going to try to get enough juice into it to fire the APU and electronics on the aircraft. Woody sampled the fuel. There was sediment, but not too much water, so he decided that they could probably use some additive just in case.

Opie and Achilles went with College Boy back inside to find the additive. It took a little while, but they got into the supply cage with the help of bolt cutters. Inside College Boy went to work. He grabbed oil, additive, and a few tubes of odds and ends that he said they should take. They loaded it up into a cart, and made their way back to the door. Walking back out, Opie tripped and made a little bit of noise, more noise than they had made since being here. That set it off, they all heard the loud roar that came from the office area past the flight operations center. Achilles came over coms.

"We have contact, may be a runner, everyone be ready if this thing comes out after us." Under night vision, Achilles saw it, standing down a hallway looking and peering at them. It looked angry and ready to attack. Achilles raised his weapon, got a steady bead, and shot it in the head. It dropped like a sack of potatoes. They gathered the rest of their materials, exited the hangar, and pushed them to the Sherpa.

Meat was taking target practice on the advancing remaining walkers. They would just shamble toward the activity, get within a 100 to 50 meters, and he would put them down with headshots. Woody took the battery, plugged it back in, and got the Avionics online. There wasn't a checklist, but they found a -10 (Operators manual) in the cockpit. College Boy put the additive in, checked the fluid levels in both of the engines, and went back into the cockpit. They went to work going through start up procedures while the rest of the team loaded the equipment into the back of the plane.

College Boy and Woody got the APU stated and went to work on getting the plane running and ready for takeoff. Everyone else got on board, secured as much as they could, and stood by the ramp in case of any surprise visitors that made their way toward the sound. It took them a few minutes, but then Woody came across the ICS. "Good morning ladies and gentlemen, this is your captain in the flight deck. We will be ready for takeoff in just a little bit. Please say hello to your lovely flight attendants, they are here to help you with whatever you need. If they can secure the cargo ramp and make sure everyone's seatbacks and table trays are in their upright and stored positions, we will begin our trip in just a few moments." That got more than a few guffaws, and Woody being the Aviator that he was slipped right into form. He had flown on a few Sherpas and since he was a rated Aviator had been shown a few things on some of these trips.

They pulled the chalk blocks, secured the ramp, and the

Sherpa began taxiing toward the runway. There was not much of a windsock any more, merely a deteriorated dull orange remnant of what it once was.

"Hey guys," Hollywood said, "there's activity along the fence line." There were no less than a hundred undead pushing against the fence. Wherever they came from, they came fast at the sound of the airplane engines. Woody moved the aircraft into takeoff position, throttled it up to full song, and they were airborne and flying west.

The plan would be to skirt I-70 toward Denver, then turn south and make for Fort Carson. From there they could hopefully get a vehicle and make their way to Cheyenne Mountain. They were hoping to try and make contact prior to that, but it would be a while before they would be able to reach anyone if they were lucky. They would try to make it in two flights, first giving St. Louis a wide berth and trying to find fuel at the airfield on Fort Leonard Wood in Missouri. If things worked out, they would be there in four hours, and on to Colorado following that.

As they flew over Terre Haute, the scene was of utter destruction. Buildings burned, remnants of a small town that housed a few universities and large high schools. There was a horde of undead in the streets. From the air the numbers couldn't be counted, but it looked to be in the thousands. Woody said it would be a great place to drop a laser guided bomb since there was no proof of civilization there anymore.

College Boy proved to be a hell of a co-pilot. He was on the map and looking up frequencies on the PAD. They would get to 5000 feet and try to get someone on the high frequency radio. He first tried to call Camslant Chesapeake radio. Nothing, no response. Next he tried Atlas radio in the middle of the country, again, nothing. He worked down a list, tried around ten and was able to find nothing but his own voice. Woody had an idea. There was a counter narcotics operation in the Bahamas, they could have coms, maybe since they were on islands they hadn't been exposed. Woody couldn't remember the name of the specific location, but Moon was able to procure the frequency from the Pad. College Boy went to work. "Opbat radio, Opbat radio, this is Seeker, do you read, Over?" There was no response, he tried again and got the same, they were starting to look at the next option, and then they got a response.

"Seeker, Seeker, this is Mustang, do you read? Over," came an excited voice.

"Roger, Mustang, this is Seeker, we are trying to make contact with any element of command and control, Over." College Boy looked over at Moon who gave him a thumbs up.

"Seeker, stand by for Mustang 06, Over."

Woody let Achilles know that they were in contact with someone, and Achilles came to the cockpit.

"Seeker 06, this is Mustang 06, who the hell are you and what are you doing on this frequency! Over."

Achilles put the mic to his mouth and spoke. "Mustang, this is Seeker 06, I am part of the Seeker element. We have been on mission in the Midwest and out of contact since things went wrong, we have requisitioned an aircraft and are trying to link up with whatever is left of the Government, Over."

"Seeker, what is your current sitrep? Over."

"Mustang, we are in the air and heading west, we have appropriated an aircraft and you are the first people we have found to be monitoring any frequencies, Over."

"Seeker, good copy, we also just stumbled upon your radio call, we monitor high freq since that is all that works since we lost most of the satellites. Have you been in contact with anyone from your command since the bombings? Over."

"Mustang, we have been out of contact since before, we have been fighting our way cross country and are trying to link up with command at Cheyenne, Over."

"Seeker, if you have the appropriate authenticators you can reach them on Atlas Radio, it is only up for six hours per day, 1400 to 2000 hrs daily, until that time we can flight follow, just need you to ident, does your transponder work, Over."

"Transponder is operational, we will squawk 1200 and ident, Over." Woody put the frequency in, and did as Achilles had told Mustang 06.

"Seeker, roger, we have your location, we will follow you as much as we can, be advised heading west, St. Louis is a hot zone, stay clear, fallout from the strikes is very bad, irradiated walkers and runner are twice as fast and deadly. From what we have gathered you should stay clear, we will relay your info to Cheyenne, also go up on Atlas at 1400, you should be able to contact if HF is good today, how copy, Over?"

"Good copy Mustang, we are heading west toward Fort Leonard Wood Airfield or whatever regional field we can find with fuel, any sitrep on our route? Over."

"Seeker, not much to tell, avoid areas of mass concentration, St. Louis and Denver are gone and radiation levels are high, we will flight follow every 30 mics, Over."

"Good copy Mustang, thanks for the heads up and help, Over." Achilles leaned back and smiled in relief.

The team continued to head west, they had roughly eight hours of fuel, and provided the headwind that they were flying into, avoiding St. Louis and getting into Missouri shouldn't be a major problem. Hollywood was teaching and flying at the same time. College Boy was proving to be a good student, and Hollywood made him do most of the flying while he was working the map. The team was moving west at around 180 knots, Woody kept them between 4500 and 6000 feet. Going higher didn't seem to provide them with any advantage, and with the quality of the fuel that had sat in the tanks, he didn't really want to have to glide down and try to land on a highway from a higher altitude.

CHAPTER 11
CONTACT

At 1400, Woody tuned Atlas radio back up. The radio was full of a plethora of activity, situation reports were coming in and out. They listened intently and waited for a break in communications to try to make contact with someone from the government. From what they could tell, elements in Alaska were not very susceptible to the undead, temperatures pretty much put a damper on undead movement. During the warmer months they had issues to deal with. High frequency communications came in from at least twelve different elements to Cheyenne control. There looked to be at least more of the government than they had assumed, but people had survived through disasters throughout history, the end of the world really seemed to be another stepping stone.

There was a break in the com traffic, and Achilles got a nod from Woody and took his turn. "Cheyenne control, Cheyenne control, this is Seeker 06, I am trying to make coms with Honcho 06, I can identify via code if need be, Over."

"Seeker 06, this is Cheyenne, we need you to identify via code, Honcho 06 is waiting, Over."

"Cheyenne control, this is Seeker 06, I identify with Seeker, Code Word Achilles, Over."

"Seeker 06, Honcho 06, damn glad to hear your voice! Is your team still intact? Over." Honcho's familiar, gruff voice coming over the com was very welcome to the whole team.

"Honcho 06, that is affirmative, team intact plus one, Over."

"Seeker 06, that is great news, sorry we could not rendezvous, we have received your information from Mustang, be advised that Leonard Wood is not safe. I need a no B.S. answer as to how far you can make it with the fuel that you have? Over."

"Honcho 06, stand by, Over."

Woody went to work, maps were flying, airspeed was being calculated as well as fuel burn rate, and he looked to be right back in his aviator element. He advised Achilles that they could make it to Dodge City Regional Airport in Kansas.

"Honcho 06, this is Seeker 06, we can make it as far as Dodge City Regional Airport, providing no issues with our aircraft, Over."

"Seeker 06, good copy, we will have an element there waiting on you, there are undead in that area, it is out of the safe zone, be advised that it could be a hot LZ (Landing zone) and we will be there, how copy, Over?"

"Good copy, we will be ready, Over."

"Seeker 06, good copy, out." Honcho signed off.

The rest of the team was briefed, one great thing was that Honcho 06 was on the other end of the communication. The idea of the plane had been awesome, this team knew what to do, and how to do it. Hopefully adversity and Mr. Murphy wouldn't keep them from the rendezvous.

The route took them south of St. Louis by over 50 miles, GPS seemed to be working, or at least trying to work. The wind was slowing them down, but Woody was pretty certain that they would be able to make it to Dodge City. Achilles thought about it, and the team had started to joke about things like "I hope the sheriff doesn't take our guns", all references to Westerns that had been remade. The rest of the flight would take about another hour and a half. Some of the guys got some shut eye, some of them looked out the windows at swarms of undead that moved across the plains looking like cattle. Almost every town that they passed looked deserted, they thought they could see places that looked active, but without landing to check them out, there was no proof of survivors anywhere.

Maybe when they got to Cheyenne they could get a better situation report, maybe some people they knew had made it out, maybe hundreds of other questions. The team felt a little stoic, they were finally going to get linked up with people that hopefully had answers. Achilles was sure that they would be part of something, something bigger than they were part of prior to the way the world was now. It had been four days for them, a lot longer for everyone else. To the team, the transition was bad, but probably even worse for people who had to mourn the end of what they knew as life, the end of relationships, families, and everything that they knew.

The rest of the flight went by, a few times the engines sputtered, Woody had to adjust the richness of the fuel, and at times had to feather the controls to keep them airborne. He joked how easy it was to fly now, no more no fly zones, no traffic patterns, no other aircraft to run into.

They were about 125 nautical miles outside of Dodge City when the next update came in from Cheyenne. "Seeker 06, Honcho 06, do you copy? Over."

"Roger Honcho 06, good copy, we are 125 nautical miles from the LZ, we are close on fuel but Hollywood is convinced that we can make in safely, Over."

"We have you on radar, be advised it will be tomorrow morning prior to exfill, best advice is to find a secure building and wait for the cavalry, there are numerous undead in the area, we will keep eyes on you via drone, how copy my last? Over."

"Good copy Honcho 06, we will make for the tower or a hangar, out."

Achilles briefed the team, they would hit the ground, taxi close to the tower, try to gain entry, clear the structure, secure the Sherpa, and wait for the cavalry. The fact that Honcho had mentioned cavalry was good. There was an old cavalry unit (helicopters) at Fort Carson near Cheyenne and Colorado Springs. Maybe they would get picked up and possibly get a nice easy flight to the link up. They hoped that it would be easy, but they all knew things go wrong during missions, so getting their hopes up was kind of a moot point.

Woody was trying to judge the wind and had descended to around 1000 feet. After making a pass of the airfield and seeing numerous undead outside of the fences, he decided that an approach that would get them to the tower and close to the hangar was the best option. Woody and College Boy brought them in for a landing, it wasn't the smoothest or the most picture perfect, but they got them onto the ground. Besides, any landing that you could walk away from was a good landing, Woody said.

Woody taxied the plane to where the wing was almost touching the door to the tower. Towers were great places to try to hole up in. They had a 360 degree field of view, usually only had one door, and were very secure locations. They dropped the ramp, did a quick version of the manuals shut down procedures, and brought the engines to a stop. Meat, Achilles, Opie, and Moon went down the ramp, weapons ready, and looked about the area. The door was right off to the left side of the plane. The approached it, and could see that in marker the words "Key on top of doorframe" had been written in what looked like a real hurry. The team kept security on the location. Undead were seen pushing on the fence closest to their location, and Achilles reached up and grabbed the key.

The key worked, well at least it opened the lock. Achilles

could tell that it hadn't been used in quite some time. They got into the building and Moon and Opie went to work clearing the stairwell. The rest of the team gathered the gear sans the toolbox and cams of lubricant and oil from the plane and waited at the door. It took Moon and Opie a few minutes to come back across the radio with the all clear. "Boss," said Moon, "it's clear, we have some journal entries on paper up here, better come up and take a look." Achilles and the rest of the team brought the gear inside and secured the door. Inside there was a steel bar to place so the door couldn't be opened, and they used it.

Everyone had taken their stuff and went up to the Observation level. The view was good, they could see the masses of undead that had gathered and were pushing at the fences. They would need to watch this closely for when their ride showed up. It was going to be a long night, it always tended to feel like that when you were waiting to be extracted following a mission. They set a guard rotation, but probably no one would be able to sleep with the growing sound of moans that the undead were producing. Moon brought the journal over to Achilles, and told him that they had eyes on the drone that Honcho had told them would be there. He also said that most of these places had backup generators and maybe they could get some air flowing since it was hot as hell inside of the tower. Meat got a few windows to open, and they had opened the hatch to the roof.

The journal was an interesting read, at least it would provide the team with a written observation of what had come to be in the days and weeks up to and following the day of reckoning.

The journal read as follows:

December 12, 2011

I don't know if anyone will ever read this, but I think it is best to keep a journal at this point. The outbreak in Korea is said to be getting worse. The President came across the news last night and told the nation that the UN Security Council had decided to make tactical strikes against North and South Korea. The decision was tough, you could tell. The President had to stop talking a few times during the broadcast. He thanked the soldiers and their families from our own military for their service in South Korea and safeguarding the 38th parallel. The decision had been made that their sacrifice was needed to save the world. Funny, I never thought that we would kill our own troops.

December 13, 2011

We don't really know what happened, it appears that we were attacked by North Korea here in the United States. The government is scattering, people are trying to fly toward Canada and even get into Mexico. From what spotty news we can get on the radio we know that most of our large cities have been taken out by nuclear strikes from North and South Korea. There are images online of Koreans killing American soldiers, it's pure chaos. The phones are no longer working, I can't get a cellular signal, and have no way to contact my family. No one came to relieve me at work this morning.

December 19, 2011

It's been days since I have seen or heard anyone, maybe I am a coward for staying here in the tower. I have food and it is secure. The internet and power are spotty. It appears that there are zombies running around the nation. The military is standing their ground and trying to get as many people that they can find who aren't infected by the undead into safe places. I heard that all survivors should head for the closest military base. I have seen some helicopters and tracked some military aircraft but no one will respond to my calls on any frequency. The last plane left here 3 days ago, A Pilot got some people that had bunched up in the hangar and took off for the North. Canada will let anyone come, they are a little better off according to what news I can find. The cold appears to affect the zombies and they don't seem as dangerous. Only parts of Canada appear to have been hit by the nukes. I haven't heard from my wife or family for days, I only hope that they are safe.

December 25, 2011

Merry Christmas, or should I say that it isn't very Merry. I have no more food, my only option is to leave and try to make it to the house. I have no idea if my family is alive. I thought they would come to get me, but they haven't. I am leaving this journal to let anyone out there know that I tried to maintain the tower. The key is above the door. Please clean up after yourselves. ....

The team all read the note, at least the guy had the gumption to lock the place up. No matter what had happened, this information was sinking in. They all thought about their parents, siblings, and friends that they probably would never see again. It was just part of the way things were, you couldn't fix it, you just had to accept it and deal with it.

Nighttime came and went, the moans kept everyone awake, or semi-awake throughout the night. When first light came, they could see the number of undead had multiplied. There looked to be at least three to four hundred of them out at the fence, and it looked like it was going to give way. They could play it one or two ways. Wait for rescue, start to take them out, or just wait and see what happened. They were secure and even a thousand of the undead couldn't push the tower over. They would have to fight their way through to whoever their rescuers were, but that would be measured upon when they showed up. Moon had the power going and the tower had HF, they tried to contact Cheyenne on Atlas but got nothing. They went back to the Opbat frequency and were able to raise Mustang. The team was advised that the last thing that Mustang had heard from Cheyenne was that they were to be picked up around 0800 hrs.

At 0750 hrs the team went back to the door, well everyone except Woody and his Barrett on the roof. They placed a VF-17 panel on the roof of the Sherpa so that if their help came they could spot the team. The undead swelling against the fence was intense. The runners actually looked as if they were coordinating the pushing. The fence was giving way, and the team had a scant 200 meters of grass between themselves and the undead masses. That is when they heard it, the sounds of a Chinook helicopter, maybe more than one. They were coming from the west, and hopefully would be on time. Achilles wasn't sure how long the fence would hold. "Woody, start taking out runners, they look to be coordinating the action. I didn't know these things could function like that!" With that Hollywood started to pick his targets, they were dropping but the intensity of the undead seemed to pick up with the resurgence of the noise.

At exactly 0800 hrs they came, two Chinooks and another beautiful sight, a AH-64 Apache attack helicopter. Achilles got coms and was told to keep his team near the tower to avoid collateral damage. The Apache peeled off in an arching turn, and the first Chinook came and landed about 300 feet from the tower. The ramp was down and a Crew member was waving to the team to hurry up. They gathered their stuff, waited on Woody to join them. Then they secured the door and placed the key back on the ledge where they had found it, and beat feet to the helicopter. They got to the ramp and could see the Apache start its gun run. It was marvelous to watch the undead be torn apart, but then again, they were once humans, so that kind of stuck at you from the inside. The team's extraction was almost anticlimactic, it went so smoothly.

The flight to Cheyenne was a little more than an hour. The team sat back, got handshakes from members of the crew, and tried to relax for the first time in a few days.

They made their final approach to a pad that looked to be near the mouth of a cave. The giant door to Cheyenne Mountain was open, and there was a flurry of activity outside on the ground. The Chinook landed, the team walked down the ramp, and saw Honcho standing about 50 feet outside of the rotors of the aircraft.

President Striker was there, along with a few members that looked to be staffers and other types that gravitated toward whoever was in charge. The Chinook took off and the officials walked toward the team. They all saluted the President and Honcho. The President shook each of their hands and told them, "Welcome back, and to your new home for a while." He then gave Honcho a nod, and walked back into the depths of the mountain complex.

Honcho had a smile on his face bigger than anyone could have imagined. "Damn boys, you made it, thank the good Lord that you made it!" He told them to get their gear and follow him inside. They would be debriefed immediately and then everything would be explained as best as the Old General could explain it. There wasn't any need for individual debriefs like in the old days, they all sat at a long table together. Honcho introduced a few new members to the team. The National Security Advisor, not the same man as when they started their mission, the director of what was now being called the Intelligence Agency, and another General named John Jackson. They all knew him as the former Colonel that was in charge at McDill Air Force Base. He had been a big shot in SOCOM, so they all had seen or met him before.

Over the next two hours Achilles spelled out the mission with help from the rest of the team: The fact that Tinker was still on duty at Atterbury, the commune outside of Greencastle, the Sherpa that they had appropriated, numbers of undead and swarms that they had seen in the air, contact with the Mustang element, and the condition of things that they had seen. They even had the idea to use the device to travel back and fix everything that had happened.

It was Honcho's turn. He went over the events of the outbreak. They were pretty sure that it was an experiment gone bad, initiated from hierarchy in North Korea. From what they had gathered they figured that once the virus was loose it spread over the entire peninsula in a matter of days through the water. The virus was actually put into the missiles that the North had fired and spread to every continent like a wild fire. The U.S. was nothing like it once had been. Over 98% of the population had been infected or killed by the blasts. Of course that was their best estimate due to the resources that they had at their disposal. Outlying places such as the Bahamas and other island communities were relatively safe, they still had three carrier battle groups that had been at sea since it all happened. Most of the big shots had made it to the complex at Cheyenne. As soon as the strike had been ordered, all of the key personnel had been shipped to Cheyenne to ride out the aftermath of the destruction that had followed. It looked as if every major country in the world was dealing with the same problems, some better, some worse.

The team took the briefing in stride. It was looking as if they were probably stuck in this version of reality forever. Honcho explained that since the security regarding the time machine no longer mattered, they had got the technology from an alien craft that had crashed in the dessert in the 1950's. It had taken the government that long to get it to work, and that is why they had just started to experiment with it a few months before the team started their mission. That made Achilles ask the question, "OK, why don't we just fire it up, go back in time and stop this whole mess before it happens?" Honcho went on to ask if they had noticed that the device was no longer there when they had come through? None of them really remembered seeing it. He elaborated by saying that they had moved it to just outside of Washington D.C., that they were going to keep the program going, but after the strikes and the fact that D.C was wiped off of the face of the planet, that the technology no longer existed.

The rest of the brief took a somber turn as the team realized they were forever stuck in this reality. They were told that the rest of the members of Darkstar were no longer with them. They had been at the facility and it had been destroyed with the rest of rural

Virginia. They, the scientists, and all of their knowledge. Honcho and his men had access to backups and schematics of the device, but no way to even begin to replicate an alien technology. Time travel was now just a dream, and one that only five people and a few laboratory animals had had the chance to experience. The team took it all in stride, except for College Boy. He looked perplexed and bewildered at all of it. That was Achilles' time to tell Honcho about the young man, and how valuable he had been to the team. The General acknowledged him, told him not to worry about not being able to report to his unit, and that God had kept him there to help the team.

Honcho kept the brief going. The President and his advisors, including himself, thought the best option was to try to get to the Former North Korea and find some sort of cure or vaccine for the undead. Now that the Seeker team had showed up, and as Honcho put it, right about when they were expecting them to show up, they might have a shot at putting together a mission to get them over there to do some scouting. Honcho told them about the contacts with Europe and other countries of the world, that there were still doctors and researchers possibly out there, and that they had a team right here with them that conducted tests and experiments that they hoped one day would help mankind out. Members of the CDC had been airlifted out prior to the strikes, and they still continued their work. Fort Carson was still operational; many people had remained after everything had happened. It was cold and that helped to stop the virus and carriers when it all came down. They had fortified it since that dreaded day had happened. It was a great place to have, but as far as every other major base in the U.S., they were gone, run over by undead.

Achilles and the team were assigned a berthing place inside of the facility. They were shown around and even had the chance to see Mr. Black again. This time he said just to call him Steve, or Agent Brooks. All the NSA cloak and dagger stuff was long forgotten about. The team had the rest of the night to relax, try to refresh their brains for the next coming days of briefings, mission planning, and whatever else Honcho could come up with. Achilles took the time to get some sleep. He was surprised how little his old shoulder injury had affected him. After all, he had only been out of the hospital for a short period of time. He guessed that the time that he had spent on mission had provided a little bit of relaxation. The shoulder was sore, but so were other parts of his body. As he drifted off to sleep, he thought about his life. He would have to find out more about the team, he would use the next few months to learn everything that he could about each and every one of them. Then his thoughts turned towards his family.

Chapter 12
Reflection

Ryder J. Mountjoy was born and raised in Thunderbolt, GA. He was one of three children that the Mountjoys raised. He had a pretty normal childhood. He went to parochial school, played sports, dated girls, and longed to be in the Army just like his father before him. He had a younger brother and sister, who knows what had happened to them and his parents, or for that matter what had happened to his daughter. He hoped one day that he would be able to find them safe and sound. He dreamed that his dad had fortified the family beach house at Tybee Island, and was using his resourcefulness to keep the family safe.

Ryder's dad was very proud to have served in the Army. He was an enlisted man and in Aviation, spent two tours in Vietnam, and loved his country. He was a staunch Republican, kept his political views out of the open, and taught the young man things that would lead him to become a special operations soldier. At a young age he taught him to hunt and skin animals. The value of a clean kill, and hunting from the ground and not in tree stands. They spent many weekends camping and doing the sorts of things that led naturally to a love of the outdoors and the need to stay out from behind a desk.

During high school, Ryder attended an All Boys,

Catholic/Military School in Savannah. This is where ROTC and leadership fit right into his mold. Sports were fun, he enjoyed the competition, but loved the military training that he received while at school. With the help of his teachers and the backing of his parents he applied to West Point. His grades were good, his moral and ethics were good, and his appointment came as no surprise to anyone in his family.

West Point was hard and fun at the same time. He always laughed when people referred to it as the "South Hampton Institute of Technology" or The Shit! That made him smile. He was selected to become an Infantry Officer, attended Jump School and the Air Assault Course while on summer training cycles at Fort Bragg and Fort Campbell. He graduated close to the top of his class, excelled at training, and loved his time there.

Upon graduation, he went to the Officers Basic Course at Fort Benning, and was selected to go to 1st Ranger Battalion, 75th Ranger Regiment as a platoon leader. His time there was great. He was at home, and even had a daughter with a woman that he never got around to marrying. They remained great friends, and he loved his time there. He went to Iraq and Afghanistan as a Platoon Leader, lost men, made friends, and was mentored by great Non-Commissioned Officers while being stationed at Hunter.

He loved his life as a Ranger, he had his tab and his combat scroll, but knew that there was more to do in the Army. He then decided to apply for Special Forces Training at Fort Bragg. Selection had been tough, but he loved every bit of it. He graduated and was assigned to 7th Special Forces Group. Being at Fort Bragg offered him the opportunity to go to many schools and different types of training. He ate it all up. He got promoted to Captain under the zone, and then applied to go to DELTA.

The DELTA selection was one that he could have never believed the Army allowed. He was sent to a land navigation course in the middle of the mountains. He walked for days, his feet were mush, did what he was told, and at the end received a certificate for the Advanced Land Navigation Course. That was it, no appointment, no acceptance. He was told 'thank you' for his time, and sent back to his unit. It was the first time that he didn't graduate at the top of an Army class and get his choice of what to do next. He was sent back to his unit, and took his role as a team leader.

A month later, Cpt. Mountjoy was sitting at his apartment one night when a knock came at the door. He got up, answered it, and was basically taken hostage. It was a crazy night, interrogation, beatings, taken to one place or another, questions, and then he was taken into a room and greeted by a man wearing civilian clothes.

He was told that this interview would decide what his future held for him in the Army. After thousands of questions, a polygraph, and even a written essay, he was left in the room. He still was unsure how long he spent in that room, but eventually a door opened, he was introduced to his new Commander, and welcomed into the greatest secret fighting force in the United States Military and even the world. He was a member of DELTA.

Missions while with DELTA were crazy, the men were all so good at their jobs, they went all over the world, participated in take down, hostage extraction, rescues and even things that no one would ever admit to. He loved his team and guys. He had been with them for two years, and that was when he was wounded in Afghanistan. The Mission was one that was supposed to be cake, they were to infiltrate the Taliban area of Afghanistan, use cover and concealment, and try to take down Bin Laden. No one officially could tell them if he was really even alive, but the intel that they were given was top notch. Mountjoy and his 5 man team were going to go in, capture him, take out any resistance, and call in for exfill. Everything worked like it should have. They were right on target, thought they had eyes on the target, and that is when the shit hit the fan. They were engaged from all sides, the locals alerted the Taliban, and they fought for over five hours. They were out of ammunition when they were finally extracted, and the target had gotten away. That is how he ended up at Walter Reed and was rehabbing his injured shoulder. It had been a dangerous mission, but at least the entire team had survived. During his musings about his family and his past, Cpt. Mountjoy, now known as Achilles, felt into the first restful slumber in days.

At 0600, Achilles was awoken by Moon who told him they were needed at a briefing in 30 mikes, and that he had slept through the entire night. The rest of the team was getting ready, they left most of their gear in the room, and went to the next briefing. Achilles could hardly believe that the last week of his life had been three years for most of the people that they were now here with. He hoped that they had decided on a next step of action, sitting and waiting never really helped a bad situation, but where would the government start? So many question, so many probabilities.

The briefing room was filled with no less than thirty people. It was large, but most of the key players that were still with the government were at the meeting. The President himself led it, dressed in ACU pants and a navy blue golf shirt with the Presidential Seal on it. This was probably the most relaxed that any member of the military would ever see an United States President. Achilles knew that things were bad, and the appearance of the President solidified that thought.

The briefing was one that encompassed the situation of the entire United States. The President, his advisors, members of the CDC, NASA, and every organization that had gotten members to Cheyenne had all their respected representatives at the meeting. The map of the United States showed major cities, red for the ones that had been hit, green for those that had populations that still held out against the undead, and yellow for those that no one had any intel about. Most of the information was gathered by either of the three carrier groups that were still at sea. They had been lucky and never gotten any infected on board. They were the command and control for aircraft and survivor groups.

Food and supplies were ferried from the places that they government still controlled. During the briefing the team learned that they had the three groups, one off the Atlantic, one in the Gulf of Mexico, and one off the coast of California. They also learned that Fort Drum in New York, Fort Greely in Alaska, and Fort Lewis in Washington State were still holding their ground. That meant that at least some of the military was still there, and maybe there was hope to deal with the undead. Contact throughout the rest of the world was spotty, England and other allies in Europe were dealing with the same problems, and places such as Hawaii and other islands seemed relatively unaffected. The breakdown of structure and everyday things such as flying had happened so fast that at least they were able to contain the spread of this virus. That was the one bit of good news, the problems was that most of the population of any of these countries lived on the mainland.

The President continued his brief, talked with each leadership team that was at the briefing and eventually came to Honcho. "General, what is your update of the proposed mission?" asked the President.

"Sir, I have been speaking with Dr. Rodney Dennis of the CDC, he believes that our best option would be to get a vaccine, to possibly infiltrate North Korea and try to find a lab. It will be dangerous, we aren't sure how bad the fallout is, nor how many infected survived the blasts. We think that we could put a team in, try to get them close enough to make it on foot to where we suspect the labs to be, maybe even find Patient One, or get some information from their computers if any are left. Then we'll extract the team and get the information back here, and then see if we can develop a vaccine. There is no cure for those infected, they are essentially dead, just the virus keeps them reanimated and moving.

Short of moving everyone to the North or South Pole, there is no way that we can keep ourselves safe without a vaccine."

The President took the news in stride. Dr. Dennis took the time to go over the virus. Most people in the room knew about it, but for members of Achilles' team it needed to be brought back out into the open.

"The flesh eater project was initiated by the North Korean Government. They were trying to contain the bird flu, but found a virus that could turn its victims essentially into zombies. They inflicted it onto their own soldiers and population through the water. This is also how it spread to South Korea. They tried to create a super soldier, but never thought about how to control it. The strain we are referring to is the Z-865 strain. That is the technical name for it. We got some early information about how and where it was being made by a deep cover operative, we lost communications with him after the tactical strikes. We know this much. When someone is infected, they have about 8-16 hours before they die of fever and choke on their own blood. They then reanimate about 4 hours later. All these reanimations want to do is eat human flesh. They are attracted to sound and smell from what we can tell. You can be infected by a bite, scratch, and possibly their mucus. The ones that appear to be runners are the ones that have contracted it via the airbursts. Walkers seem to have been bitten or scratched. We can tell everyone this much, from our research, the runners appear to have the ability to reason and be rather resourceful. They seem to be able to get walkers to follow and do what they want them to do. We aren't sure if this is via sound or some sort of mental link, but we are experimenting with the ones that we have locked up at Carson."

The President thanked everyone for attending the briefing, and asked Honcho and the team minus Basse to remain behind. Basse had been assigned to the airfield at Fort Carson, and seemed rather happy to be back in the Air Force. The President started by sitting down in a chair and asking everyone to gather around.

"Gentlemen, I can't begin to say how proud I am that you made it to us. The fact that the experiment worked, and you were able to rendezvous with us is astonishing. I knew that the team was top notch, but the resilience that you have shown in amazing. We have been telling everyone that we could make this new mission a go, provided that we could put together a team, and it looks like we have the team here to get the mission started. I think that the General will fill you in on the rest of the details, but what I need is for you to think of anything, or any questions that you need answered prior to departing on yet another suicide mission. I know that it will be dangerous, and I know you used to get paid to do that sort of thing, but now, will you do it for your country and for all of humanity?"

The question that the team faced was a big one. They looked at each other, then back to the President and all nodded that they would do what needed to be done. "Good, then I won't stop you from getting underway. We would like to be operational in less than a week if possible. I know for you men that is a short time, but for the rest of us, it's been a long time since we have been basically marooned here." With that, the President shook their hands and left the room.

Honcho closed the door and let out a sigh. "Well men, what do you guys think?" It was a big question, in fact there were so many questions. Could they do this, was there a cure, what obstacles would they have to get through, the questions that they all thought about were monstrous, but then again, most of them had been on missions that had problems from the start. They were good, and they would have to plan and execute to try to save mankind.

"North Korea, well, we think that there are still people running whatever is left of that country. They were prepared for the strikes, and we think that their President is still alive and running the show," Honcho said. "Our initial plan is to get you guys to link up with our Pacific Strike Group near Baja. It will be the first hurdle. We lack the ability to get you all the way there via airplane; we can get you to about 100 miles from where they can extract you via a Marine Osprey. The crossing will be tough, but there should be a limited amount of undead to deal with. From there you will make the eight day journey to just outside of North Korea. We think we can get you to about 50 nautical miles from the mainland. From there we will have to airdrop you onto or as near to the mainland as possible. We aren't too sure about the amounts of undead that you will face on the Korean Peninsula, the amounts range from many hundreds to thousands. Nukes didn't really take them out as we expected. Sure, those close enough to the impact sites were obliterated, the others just seemed to get stronger. You won't have much in the way of coms except for a limited amount of time each day. The good thing is, we think that the research facility is close to the DMZ (Demilitarized Zone) in the city that really never housed anything, or at least that is what we thought. We have a few scientists here that we would like for you to take a look at, none have any military experience, but some were quite adventurous in their former lives. Having one with your team is a must, he or she will be the one to try to get enough information that we can try to start on a vaccine. Then, the hardest part, exfilling back to the Strike group. We know that near their naval bases they have all sorts of subs or mini-subs. We are thinking they might be the best way off of the mainland, or you might even have to appropriate some kind of boat."

The plan looked good on paper. The team would have the next five days to look though the plans, make changes, find a scientist that could do what they needed, but also wouldn't be such a drain on the team that said scientist would jeopardize the mission. Achilles took the chance to assign jobs to the team. Moon and Opie would take a look at their technology, get together items that they would need or that could help them to make the mission a success. Hollywood would coordinate with the Carrier Group, and also with the aircrew that would get them as close to the pickup as possible. He was also tasked with transportation from point A to point B. Meat and Achilles would continue with planning the mission, and also selecting a scientist to go with them on this little expedition.

Achilles and Meat started by asking for personnel files on the scientific team that was at Cheyenne Mountain. They read and sifted through all the files that they had. After what seemed like hours Meat stumbled across a file that might just prove to be the most helpful. One of the team that worked at the CDC wasn't prior military, but had a few distinct characteristics that would be very helpful to the team. He was a former marksmanship champion that had finished just out of the medals at the Beijing Olympics in 2008. He was a damn awesome shot with a pistol, and was a backup as a rifle shooter. He was a scientist, a biological chemist with a background in adventure sports. According to this man's file he was a civilian skydiver, scuba certified, and loved the outdoors. This was their man, now just getting him to agree to the mission would be the hard part.

Moon and Opie did their job well. They met with members of the Armed Forces and the Intelligence communities. They learned that most of the satellites were still operational, and they could be controlled from Cheyenne. The international Space Station was still operational, and they now launched rockets from Alaska to transfer the astronauts in and out. It sucked, but they did their job by keeping what they could operational up in space. One of the most valuable things that Moon and Opie came across during their research was a synthetic fuel source that could help to purify fuel that was left in full trucks or in gas tanks of vehicles that had sat dormant for a significant period of time. They coordinated with the Armed Forces and now had the ability to call in airstrikes from drone aircraft via the PADS that they carried, and even got as much current intelligence updated as the memory on their devices could carry.

Hollywood set up the transport from Cheyenne to Gila Bend in Arizona. From there they would make their way via ATV's that were modified for efficiency and sound suppression. They would make their way to the coast in Mexico and link up with a Marine Osprey to take them to the USS Chung Hoon, an Aegis class destroyer that was with what was left of the Pacific Fleet. From there they would make the eight day crossing and then jump into North Korea, or the former North Korea, via HALO jump. The jump was planned for nighttime to avoid being seen, and also so that any undead wouldn't be able to see their parachutes. He had been guaranteed that their GPS would be operational the entire time they were en route cross country to the link up with the Destroyer.

Achilles and Meat took the time to go and meet up with the scientist. He was brought into the briefing room by Mr. Black and was greeted by Honcho.

"Dr. Baker, do you know we have asked you to come here today?"

Baker responded that there was some scuttlebutt about a mission, and that they needed a scientist to go with the group of Army guys that would be going to North Korea.

"Good, my men have sifted through everything, and they think that you may be the best option. This is Col. Achilles, and Major Meat, they are leading the mission and they would like to bring you up to speed. You by no means have to accept the mission, and I would like for you to hear them out prior to saying yes or no." Baker nodded his head, and said he was all ears.

Achilles went over the brief beginning with takeoff from Cheyenne to how they would get onto the North Korean mainland. He told Baker how they had evaluated him from his file, how much his personal skills could help the mission succeed, and that they needed him. Dr. Baker weighed it all, he looked at the plan, laughed a little, and told them that he would need to think about a few things. He was also concerned that he wasn't the smartest person when it came to zombies, and that there were other people that knew more than he about the subject. Achilles looked the man over, he was slightly overweight, wore glasses, and seemed to be a little unsure of himself.

"Let me ask you a question, do you think that you can follow our orders?"

"Yes, of course," Dr. Baker said, adjusting his glasses.

"Do you think that you can get what the rest of the scientists need to make this happen if we help you?"

"Yes."

"Are you scared shitless about any part of this mission?"

"Yes," he smiled nervously. The rest of the team laughed in acknowledgment.

"Then, Dr. Baker, I really think that you are our man. I don't want to put words in your mouth, I'm not going to fill you with any false hope, but what I can guarantee you is this, if you come with us, do what my men tell you to do, and use that ability you have with guns, parachuting, and science, my men and I will be a lot better prepared than we would be if we have to take some lab doctor that has no clue about firearms and real life scenarios. Take the night to let us know what your answer is. I need an answer tomorrow at 0700 hrs. We begin final mission preparation then, and I need my whole team together to do that." Achilles shook Dr. Baker's hand, and with that Dr. Baker left the room.

Honcho stayed for a few hours and talked with them about the rest of the mission. They got frequencies, times when they would be in the dark as far as radios and communications, and the best up to date intelligence on the situation in North Korea. The team spent the rest of the night getting things together, repacking their gear, and putting together gear for Dr. Baker. They were pretty sure that he was the guy, he just needed to figure it out for himself. Achilles had no doubt in his military mind that this man would be coming with them.

At 0700 hrs Achilles and Honcho were waiting in the briefing room with the President. They were going over the final draft of the mission, and when they would initiate the countdown to get everything moving. Dr. Baker came in right on time. He was wearing a pair of woodland camouflage pants, brown shirt, and had his backpack with him.

"Good morning, Dr. Baker," the President said. "I see that you have your gear, does this mean you will be joining the team?"

"Yes sir!" was all that he said.

Achilles welcomed him to the team, called Meat to come and retrieve him. He then told Honcho and the President that they were a go, and that they could leave whenever they wanted to launch the mission. The outlining of the mission was as discussed before. Achilles spoke about the operational aspects, gear, armament, movement and communications. The President and Honcho went over the North Korea element, the knowledge that they had about the Ghost City as some people in the government were calling it, and the underground facility that they knew was there. It was all explained and the team was to get going ASAP. They shook hands, and the President once again thanked Achilles and told him to extend that thanks to the men on his team.

Achilles went back to the bay that they were staying in. The team was meeting Dr. Baker and they were all discussing things that normal soldiers discuss during downtime. "All right men, we are heading out in three hours, we will take the bird as far as it can take us, then we will be cross country on the ATV's. Hopefully we can rendezvous with the transport from the ship and get going across the pond as soon as possible. Dr. Baker, you will stay with Meat at all times while we move, he is your guardian angel, with that being said I know that you also have some great skills that will contribute to the success of the mission. I need you to select a codename, or call sign and then we would like to hear about you."

With that Dr. Baker turned to the team and began telling them the 411 about himself. "My name is Kristopher Baker. I am from near the Kentucky/West Virginia Border, raised in a small town that wasn't even really a town even prior to all this shit. I went to West Virginia, got a degree in Business. I went straight to grad school and then ended up going to Northwestern for medical school. After that I was recruited to work at the CDC, mainly doing things with mining operations, black lung, that sort of thing. I have always been a big fan of the outdoors, as you know I was in the Olympics as a shooter, it was cool. I have never killed a person, and for that matter never killed a zombie. I love to rappel, scuba dive, and skydive. I was married before all the world got turned upside down. No clue if she made it, but that was a while back and I have come to deal with it. I have been working on the vaccine with the team here, we don't think that we can find a cure, but we think a vaccine can be made if we get a pure enough sample of brain and lung tissue from those that were first infected. As far as a call sign, call me Stewy."

"Stewy?" said Moon.

"Yeah, a bunch of buddies playing Xbox gave me crap for always picking Stewart while we played Nascar, since then it has just been shortened to Stewy."

The team was geared up and ready to go, the Chinook was on the pad, and they loaded up the gear and SUV's. They were great models, some of the team had used them on Black Op's in Afghanistan. They were pretty much silenced, had running lights for NVG operations, and were more rugged than the ones that you bought at the local Off Road shop. They entered the bird and were off and headed west. It would be about a three hour flight, they would have time to get a little shut eye and get prepped prior to getting to the landing zone.

CHAPTER 13
THE GOVERNMENT

Back at Cheyenne, the President called Honcho into his office. They needed to have a talk, the past few days had really made things go into overdrive. Here was a team that they had actually buried, and thought were gone. They fact that the experiment worked, and they had made their way back to the remnants of the government was downright amazing. He called Honcho in and began the conversation.

"General, I can't begin to say how shocked and amazed I am that this group of soldiers made it to us. They showed their METL (Mission Essential Task List) by surviving through all of it, and then making it to us. I am just amazed by the whole situation. A few years ago when you came to me with this idea, I thought you were insane. We never thought there would be an apocalypse, nor could we conceive that North Korea had this mess in their arsenal. Now we are sending them back out and across the ocean to find a vaccine. Please, if you would, tell me more about this band of soldiers that you have put together."

"Well sir, we had gotten the mission planned, made all of the equipment work, and to be honest the entire scientific team was so far ahead of our plan that we just got things going fast. The team, well that is another matter. We had been searching high and low for people to do the mission, from NASA pilots, to shooters, to scientists. The main concern was kind of like when we first selected astronauts, we wanted the cream of the crop, but never got that far. We needed to get a group of people together that were in great shape, had knowledge of weapons, electronics, computers, and to be honest, people that could get shit done. I just happened to be in D.C for a meeting at the Pentagon when I got the call from Number One. For some strange reason she found this group, well most of them at Walter Reed for one reason or another. It made sense, but she later came clean and told me that she had arranged for all of them to be there.

Colonel Achilles was there because of wounds he received in the Mountains of Pakistan, he was chasing Taliban fighters and trying to of course find Bin Laden. He got hurt, didn't really need to be in Walter Reed, but she thought it would be the first step in getting a good group together. Major Meat, same type of deal. She just used some influence in the D.O.D and placed them all in the right place at the right time. So plain and simple, they were a unique group of people that were perfect for the mission. They even helped to find CW4 Opie, that was one piece we hadn't really even thought about. I tell you sir, they are as good of a group as any special operations team that the government has ever put together." Honcho looked pleased with himself and with the success of his team.

"General, I hope for all of our sakes that they are that good, this mission needs to be a success if we can ever start to reclaim our country from these damn zombies! This is the only real foothold that we have. Our estimates show at least a 97 percent infection rate. That leaves us with not very many damn humans left. For our allies, they are in the same or worse condition. Let's hope for the sake of all mankind that they can pull this mission off." The President stood and began pacing about the room.

Honcho said reassuring, "Sir, we will be in contact with

them throughout most of the mission. We have windows throughout the day to get their progress. As soon as they can link up with the Chung Hoon, they will be ready to make the crossing. I was thinking that maybe we can beef up the team with some of what is left of Seal Team 5 out of Pearl, but they seem to have their hands full. Our forces are keeping Hickam and Pearl secure, but the outbreak on Hawaii will soon force us to abandon it. So besides here and Alaska, we no longer control much of anything."

"OK then," the President stated, "I will need status updates in the CDC and I would like to be kept up to date with what the scientific team has going on. General, I need a no bull shit assessment, can these guys get us what we need?"

"Sir, I think that this is our best shot. The last team we sent in, they weren't the right mix, hell, who knows if they are still alive? All in all this team has a great shot at getting the samples. I feel bad about not letting them know about our first shot at getting samples, but that is need to know, just like their original mission. There is no sense in telling them that our hodgepodge group of spooks, rangers, marines, and Para rescue guys got overwhelmed. I believe that first team was just too big, too undertrained, and too freaked out. We sent them in and expected results. They weren't trained and we caused that mission to fail."

     * * *

On the Chinook the team was catching the last bit of shuteye that they would have for a day or two. Most of them didn't mind sleeping while the aircraft was moving anyway. They had been airborne for around two and a half hours when they heard the pings in the airframe. One of the crew chiefs started firing out the gunner's window with the M-240G that was mounted and the aircraft banked to the left and down in one swift motion. Achilles spoke into the mic and asked the pilots what was going on.

"Sir, we are taking a lot of small arms fire, we can't see anything but muzzle flashes, oh, shit, hang on!" The aircraft then felt like it was hit by a boulder. The pilots did a hell of a job getting them down to the ground, yelled through the mic to get unassed from the aircraft ASAP if they didn't want to return to base. With that the team was on their rides, a little shaken, but off of the Chinook within thirty seconds of hitting the ground. It seemed to last forever, but the entire course of contact lasted about three minutes.

Meat was in the lead, the rest of the team was hauling ass behind him. He headed for cover, well at least what looked like cover. They rode for a few minutes and made it to a cliff overhang, pulled the ATV's into a circle, and then formed as good of cover as they could while the Chinook disappeared out of sight. Moon had his Pad going and was trying to triangulate their position, Stewy looked like he was about to piss himself, and the rest of the team looked and listened for anything. They could hear sporadic gunfire, and even could see tracers shooting at the fleeing aircraft. Achilles heard from the pilots that they were in for a lot of company, and that they should try to hunker down.

Moon had them as best as he could figure, 150 miles from the coast, nowhere near the town they were supposedly heading for. They would have to make their way cross-country from here. They didn't have enough fuel in the ATV's for the trip, so they would have to scavenge what they could.

"So, what do you guys think?" asked Achilles. "We can wait for dark, try to get moving and avoid whatever or whoever was shooting at the bird, or we can move out now and risk being discovered. That could lead to a firefight with an unknown amount of tangos, and we could be way outnumbered." By looking around it seemed the entire group was on the same sheet of music, basically hunker down and wait for darkness, fire up the 4-wheelers, then head toward the coast.

"Sir, I have a good idea that we are right about where I thought, we can stick to the dried up river beds and head out as soon as it's goggle dark," said Moon.

It was as good an idea as any, they could hear the people in the distance, hoots and yelling like they were victorious. Why the hell would anyone shoot at an Army helicopter in the first place? Maybe they were pissed that no one had come to the rescue after the attacks. Anarchy has a way of spreading once the government is out of the picture. No way that the team could know what was out there, no idea how big the force was, no clue as to how well armed and organized the bad guys were, and this wasn't their mission. They needed to beat feet as fast as possible, live to fight another day, and then make the rendezvous.

Night seemed to take forever to come, they heard laughs and even some dogs barking. The 4-wheelers would make minimal noise, and with Stewy not being used to driving under goggles, they decided to have him ride on the back of Meat's ATV. Moon would be taking point, he would try to stick to the river beds and flats, keep it under 25 mph, and try to make as a direct route toward Baja as possible. If they were lucky, they could make 60-100 miles tonight, then find a good place to rest and send out a team to get some fuel. Most of the land was Indian Reservation, so they would have to find a village and pilfer some gas, maybe they could even find a band of survivors, which was what Achilles was hoping for.

They got moving, south by southwest and everyone knew the drill, single file, 10 meter separation, and if they made contact to fan out and form a defensive perimeter. The next contact time that they would have satellite coverage for coms was 0100 hrs. That was a good four and a half hours from the time that they set out. Moon got them going and everyone kept their heads on swivels for the first few miles. They heard some shooting, mostly just shots into the dark, some dogs barked, but they rode on through without any issues.

Achilles got the handheld GPS that was mounted on the ATV to get triangulation around 2330 hrs, they were only 10 miles off of Moon's guess. That meant they had 160 miles total to go to the rendezvous. Pad coms kept everyone in the know about the route, they had to avoid ditches, gullies, and washouts, but Moon kept the pace and everyone did a good job in following.

At 0055 Achilles called a halt; they had made it just over 55 miles. That meant they still had a ways to go, but they hoped that it would be smooth sailing from here on out. Opie got the Satcom unit out, and Achilles waited to transmit until right at 0100.

"Cheyenne, Cheyenne, this is Seeker, how copy? Over."

"Seeker, Cheyenne, we read you loud and clear, Honcho is awaiting sitrep, Over."

"Cheyenne, the bird took rounds, we have been E and E for the last few hours, position is 20 miles southwest of Elfrida Arizona, gas is almost half way, we still have 95 miles to make the rendezvous, Over."

"Seeker, be advised, you have unfriendlies in the path, large amounts of undead swarming in your path, no real safe way around... Estimated 300 to 1000 walkers... We have your beacon and UAV predator coverage for the next 5 hours... You might want to find high ground and prepare yourselves for the inevitable... Over."

"Roger, Cheyenne, any thoughts? Over."

"Hilly area near Bisbee, around 15 miles, we will hit the swarms, you will need to get eyes on and laze the targets for us, Over."

"Roger that, we will be in contact again in 30 mikes, Seeker out."

The team heard it all, Achilles got Moon to get the team moving, the instructions were simple, try to find high ground and a defensible location to deal with the swarms, they were armed to the teeth, but they hadn't really had to deal with this as of yet. Moon set a blistering pace, and they made good time to the outskirts of Bisbee.

They came to a stop around two miles from the town. They couldn't see or hear anything yet, so Achilles got Meat and Opie to go and find a good spot to set up camp. They hoped to call in the fire support and wait for the swarm to disperse or possibly move on, it was a long shot, but the team had to at least grasp some hope. They would expend most of their ammo if it came to a firefight, and from all the Intel that Stewy and the team had gathered, only head or spinal cord shots would take down the walkers. The other concern would be runners, they seemed to be smarter and the walkers would just follow the direction that they would go.

Meat and Opie were gone for what seemed like an eternity. They took one of the ATV's to save gas, and all the rest of the team could do was sit and wait. After almost an hour they heard Meat on the Pad radio.

"Boss, we have a structure, old convenience store, has gas pumps also, two doors, windows are boarded up and have steel bar reinforcement. Not sure why it's empty, we have it cleared, coordinates to follow."

Hollywood lead the team the rest of the way, they made it to the structure and parked the ATV's out by the pumps. Inside the place looked like there had been a robbery and a few homicides. They blocked the door and found the roof access. The best bet was to take positions and try to target the swarm, the only problem was the lack of swarm. They couldn't hear anything, no dogs, no shooting, no moaning, not anything but the dead silence of night. They would have UAV coverage for the next few hours, but after that, if they didn't find anything they would be on their own. Achilles sent Hollywood down to try to get the pumps going. Moon joined him and started to work on the pumps. Of course they didn't work, but Moon used the kit from the ATV with the battery and got one of them to come to life. The hum of the gas pump was all that anyone heard. They got to work fueling the ATV's while Achilles got on the Satcom and tried to raise Cheyenne once again.

"Cheyenne, this is Seeker, come in, Over."

"Seeker, we have you five by five, we also have your beacon, be advised, large mass inbound at 1000 meters, moving directly toward your position. Over."

"Roger, we will laze the mass as soon as we get contact, be advised, there are fuel tanks here, no danger close fire mission, we need 400 meters, break."

"Hollywood, you need to get a vantage point and laze the undead swarm, they are 1000 meters and closing, Over."

"Roger."

"Break, Cheyenne, did you copy my last, Over."

"Roger, we will await your laze, mass IR is available via Pad feed, Over."

"Roger, will laze when we have eyes on, anything further? Over."

"Roger, you have 30 mikes worth of voice, out."

Hollywood saw the vantage point he needed, he grabbed the laser designator, the Barrett and his M-4 and headed toward the water tower. Moon was with him, and they made their way toward it. This was crunch time for the team, Opie covered them with his M-4, but there was no need. They made their way to the tower in record time for two guys with that much equipment. Achilles could tell that the team was ready to go, even Stewy had his weapon out and was ready to take down anything that came into his view.

"Boss, this is Woody, I have the swarm, I think they were a little short on their numbers. I can't get a count, but there are at least a thousand of them. I think we might want to shoot a few to get them heading toward your location, then we can laze a building and hit them with everything that Predator has on it, Over."

"Good call, we actually think a flare might get them heading this way, I will have Opie fire a green star cluster out toward the building directly to our south, will that give you good coverage of their movement? Over," came Achilles' voice.

"Roger that, we can follow them the rest of the way in."

Opie used the star cluster, and the world came to light in the green hue that they gave off. The rest of the team still couldn't see the swarm, but Moon and Woody had a great view of them. As soon as the star cluster sent into the air, they saw the runners take off toward the light, then the walkers started to after them. Achilles got on the Satcom and told Cheyenne to relay to the operator of the drone that they were going to laze the target.

As the runners came into view, the drone dropped all of its ordinance in one pass. The night was turned into day, and the team saw parts of bodies flying and wails and moans erupt as the bombs struck home. It was a great hit, the operator of the drone brought it straight in on top of the mass, the team then went to work on what remained of the large numbers of undead heading their way. Moon and Woody were sniping from their water tower position, that was good and bad. They had a great vantage point, but then they would have to deal with unwanted company as the noise from the M-24 and the Barrett .50 brought undead to their position.

Everyone on the roof was taking shots at undead that were still coming through the fire and smoldering bodies of the undead that had fallen prey to the strikes from the Predator. Even Stewy was in on the action. Achilles came over the channel and told everyone to conserve ammo and to try to take headshots. That way they would have ammo and not be mission critical in the firepower department. The swarm, or what was left of it, split into two groups. One seemed to shamble toward the water tower, and the larger group came toward the filling station. It looked to the team as if they were dealing with a hundred and fifty or so, and they had plenty of ammo to handle that. Moon and Woody were just hoping that they couldn't climb a ladder!

The firefight went on for at least another half hour. The team had taken most of the undead out; they were sure that the noise would attract more, but they had to deal with as many as they could before they got back on the ATV's and continued to head toward the pickup. Achilles confirmed with everyone on the team an ammo count, and then had to make the call to send Opie and Meat downstairs to secure the lower level. Even though they hadn't seen any of the undead make it to their stronghold, he was sure that there would be some stragglers.

Moon and Hollywood were handling themselves with just suppressed pistols at that point. They had climbed down to about ten feet off of the ground and were taking their time in dispatching the last few around the base of the tower. Hollywood told Achilles about their situation, and then continued to shoot and reload as Moon did the same. When the mass was nothing more than a pile of bodies, they climbed to the base of the tower and started to make their way back to the station.

Opie and Meat dealt with the two that had made it into the station, they had no clue as to how they had gotten through their hail of gunfire, but they were in the station and looking for something to eat. They took them down, radioed back up to the top that it was clear, and went outside to get the 4-wheelers running. The team gathered, took a direction and heading, and split from the town just as fast as they had come in. Achilles ordered them to make a southwest heading and to find a place to hunker down for the rest of the night. They would need to ride for a while to shed off the rush that they were all feeling. Even though it was relatively an easy fight, they would all be a little jacked up from the flow of adrenaline that they had experienced over the last half hour.

CHAPTER 14
UNWELCOME COUNTRY

As they were riding out, Moon set a 40 mile per hour pace for the team to get as much distance from anything undead as possible. They were all sure that the noise had attracted anything that had separated from the main swarm, that meant that stragglers would be coming toward the noise from far and near. Woody was bringing up the rear of the single file convoy when he came over the radio.

"Shit! I have been hit, GOD DAMN my leg is on fire!"

Achilles responded, "Are you able to keep riding?"

"Yeah, yes sir!"

"Moon, find us someplace out of line of sight! And find it ASAP!"

With that Moon brought them to the gulley of a washed our river bed. The team pulled to a halt, circled the ATV's into a defensive perimeter. Moon had a great spot for them, a little overhang, everyone dismounted and Opie helped get Hollywood off of his ATV. He was hit, and no one had any clue what had gotten him. Opie went to work under red lens flashlight, he cut off the pants above the wound. Fortunately, Woody had a clean entry and exit wound. It looked like he was hit by a small caliber round, possibly a .22 or .38 caliber. They never heard a shot, but all of their ears were ringing from the gunfire they had just expended. Opie slapped him on the shoulder, told him he would be OK and went to work. The rest of the team was looking and trying to find where the shot had come from. It was strange, they knew that undead couldn't have possibly fired a gun and hit them, that meant that they had been shot by someone that was unaffected by the virus – a survivor.

After what seemed like an eternity to Woody, he was bandaged up, in a fresh pair of ACU pants, and doing his best not to complain about the gunshot. Opie had administered him some antibiotics, and given him a local to ease the pain. Achilles told him not to use any morphine, and Woody said he was good without it anyway. The team sat and listened for a while, nothing out of the ordinary occurred for quite some time. Night turned to dawn, and they still were in the defensive perimeter. The team knew that it would be a while before they had any UAV cover, and that fact made them a little leery to get moving. If they had to go during the day they could make better time, but anyone and anything would be able to see them.

Achilles took a poll. They had roughly thirty-six hours until the rendezvous, and they needed to get there in a timely manner. The mission hinged on the fact that they didn't want to go any farther on ATV than necessary. The team felt confident that they could move during the daylight hours, and getting as much distance between them and whoever took the pot shot at them was the best possible scenario. It could be part of the group that shot at the Chinook, or it could be a whole different threat. With Woody being hit, and not too much help for the group, Meat picked up the Barrett and went out of the perimeter to see what was around. Opie followed him.

Meat and Opie were using the optics from the Barrett and the spotter scope as they searched the area for any immediate threat. There looked to be some stragglers from the main group around the vicinity of the town, but there was neither hide nor hair of anyone that resembled a human. After a while they assumed it was safe, and went back to get saddled back up. The ride was going to be long, and the longer that they waited to get moving, the faster they would have to travel to get to the LZ.

They rode for about four hours and were now only about 50 miles from the LZ. Nothing out of the ordinary occurred. A few times they had to move fast to get away from a group of the undead, but other than that it was pretty smooth sailing for the team. Stewy seemed at home with the group, and his demented sense of humor kept the group laughing while they were riding. Not too much of anything else to do except to keep riding and shooting the breeze while keeping their heads on a swivel.

They reached a point in the journey where they saw a man in a truck, a beat up old Ford F-150 on a ridge line. Achilles was checking him out through his binoculars when he saw the man doing the same though a spotter scope. The man actually looked to be smiling, waved his arms in the air, and looked to wave the team in. Achilles barked out a few orders, told Opie to come with him, and told the rest of the team that if there was trouble, to make their way to the LZ and he and Opie would catch up.

Opie and Achilles approached using a trail pattern with Opie in the rear. They were under coms with the team, and it something went wrong, then they would separate and take down the man as if he were hostile. When the made their way up to him, he was sitting on the tailgate of his truck, holding a modified H&K rifle and having a dip. They approached and he sat his gun down.

"Howdy boys," the man said. "I wasn't sure if I would ever see a U.S. soldier again! I've been out here forever and all I come across are survivor groups, undead, and whatever I can scare up to eat."

Achilles greeted him. "Sir, my name is Col. Achilles, we are making our way cross-country, and you seem to be out here in the middle of nowhere, are you by yourself?"

The man laughed, and said "By myself. Naw, my son has you covered and I wasn't sure you really weren't bandits, so until we can reach a parlay, I would suggest that you don't make any sudden moves. Him and I are both ex-soldiers, and we really don't want any trouble."

Achilles took a moment, wondered to himself if this was the shooter that hit Woody, and decided that it would be better to talk than to worry about getting hit by a sniper. "Sir, I understand, we are just trying to get through here and make it to our rendezvous. We are on a mission, and we thought coming up and talking was better than exchanging shots at one another."

The man smiled, held out his hand and said "I'm Sergeant First Class (Retired) Tim Brown, was in the 101st when I was a young man, now my boy and I are just trying to stay alive out here. We made it from Indiana out here and are just following some wild game. My wife was in Los Angeles when all this bad shit went down. I know for sure she isn't with us anymore, but we thought it better to go and try to find her and my other boy than to just sit in Indiana and do nothing." He made a gesture, and just like he said, a man in a Ghillie suit about 100 meters away rose off of the ground and started walking this way.

Achilles called the rest of the team up, and they moved with the trucks and the ATV's off of the ridge line as to not silhouette themselves. They settled in to hear the Browns' story which was the same as many others: survival. Both of them had been soldiers, the son had been to Iraq and Afghanistan, and when everything went down he was in the National Guard in Indiana. He had gotten as many supplies as he could, guns, ammo, night vision goggles, and had actually been at Camp Atterbury. Their story was interesting, encounters with undead, bandits, small towns that had become fortresses, and even the loss of the young man's girlfriend. He didn't elaborate on it, but you could tell by the look in his eyes that it was going to haunt the young man for many years.

Achilles filled them in on the situation with the government, gave a little hint that they were on a mission to find a cure, and that if they wanted to travel together that it might help the father/son team make it farther west. They actually had a nice little set up, a little fortress that they had been working out of. It was a canyon area that had once housed some Native American Indians. Both of them had trucks that they had modified, and even had fuel. They spoke about some bandits that followed the zombie swarms, and even thought they might have been the ones that took pot shots at the team.

Moon came forward and informed Achilles that he had made contact with Honcho, gave a sitrep, and that they would have UAV overhead cover on and off for the next fourteen hours. Somehow they had moved some satellites around to help the team out, and they thought that it might help since their run in last night with a swarm. They got out a Pad and started plotting the next leg of the journey. The Browns had made some rabbit stew and shared it with all of the team members. Over dinner, it was the older Brown that came up with the idea. "Say, Colonel, we are just out here trying to survive, we are heading the same way, and you could use the two trucks to get where you are going faster. We can help you guys get to where you are going, combine the gas, and all we need in exchange are two of these ATV's for our trouble. It would be better for us to use these than the trucks while we are gathering food and supplies." It made total sense, they had these trucks in great shape, and the team was going to ditch the ATV's anyway at the rendezvous.

"Tell you what, Sergeant Brown, you have a deal. What I need from you is to honor your oath, do you still swear to support and defend the Constitution of the United States, against all enemies, foreign and domestic? Do you swear to honor the orders of the Officers appointed over you? Do you swear to support the

Uniform Code of Military Justice?" Both of them nodded their heads and in unison said, "We do."

With that they were both sworn in on the spot. Achilles had seen it in a movie about the crusades, even got on the radio and told Honcho that he had appointed them soldiers, restored their ranks, and promoted them right on the spot. They didn't seem to believe that there still was a president, but as the junior Brown, not a Staff Sergeant pointed out, they were the only military that still acted like military that they had seen in over three years.

With Master Sergeant Brown who was now code named Big Brown, and his son, now code named Little Brown, they selected a route, put two of the ATV's in the truck beds, mounted up, and high tailed in the direction of the rendezvous. In the first truck that Big Brown drove, Achilles rode shotgun, and Woody, Stewy, and Opie rode in the back. In the second, driven by Little Brown, Meat rode shotgun, Moon rode in the back manning the radio. The fact that he could relay from the Satcom radio to Achilles made it OK to separate the two.

As they rode, Big Brown talked about the area. He told Achilles that they had been in this area for around a year, never getting any farther and always falling back to their semi quasi compound that they had. He referred to it as unwelcome country, told him about the survival groups, radicals that had made their own armies, or as he would call them platoon size elements that took what they wanted. It was one of these groups outside of Laredo, Texas that had gotten Little Brown's wife. They had captured her while they were off hunting for food, left a note, but there was little that could be done about it. The Browns found her, raped and beaten, then hung by her neck with a taunting note pinned to the torn remnants of her shirt. He had gotten his son to control his rage, and then they systematically hunted them down and killed all of them. It was justice, and in this new world that was how you handled things.

The drive to the rendezvous was rather uneventful, they stopped and scouted a few times, even sniped a few of the undead as they were just stumbling around. Big Brown would curse as his son would mumble biblical verses while he shot them, but no one from the Seeker element said anything in response.

They arrived with ten hours to spare before the pickup. They stayed about 500 meters away from the site where the Ospreys were going to land, made contact with the Chung Hoon, and made themselves ready for the wait. Between the ship and Cheyenne, they were able to push up the pickup by about six hours, but there was still a problem with one of the two aircraft. They decided that it would be better if both aircraft launched at once, just in case of an issue. That was the plan, and the team would have to sit and wait in this area until the pickup. The good thing was that they had satellite and UAV cover for the entire time, if something bad came their way, they were in good shape. Both of the Browns decided it was a good thing to wait it out with them, and that it was their duty to make sure that the team got on board the Ospreys with no issues.

Just as they thought it would be another uneventful wait, they got a message from the team at Cheyenne.

"Seeker, this is Cheyenne, Break… Possible unfriendlies heading in the vicinity of the town from the north… Be advised, they are exchanging fire with other unfriendlies… They are five miles from your location heading right at you… Five vehicles…. behind looks to be runners being herded by motorcycles…… how copy? Over."

Achilles brought the team up to speed, Moon got on the Pad and got a visual feed from one of the two UAV's that were flying over their position. From one point of view they were far enough out of the way if they hunkered down, but as they watched the way it was developing they would have to make a choice whether or not to get involved. That is one thing that commanders of military units have always valued and hated at the same time. Surveillance from the air is one thing, facts from troops on the ground was another.

As the team used scopes, binoculars, and Pad video to see what was unfolding in front of their eyes, it quickly became clear that they either support the group running, or become trapped.

"Cheyenne, this is Seeker, we have the tally on the two elements that you have spotted. It seems to us that they are being chased down by the second group." Achilles looked grimly around at his team. They looked ready for anything.

Moon pointed out that the group that were running had women and children with them, and they looked to be running for their lives.

"Cheyenne, we are leaning toward making contact with the second group to give the first group a chance, how copy? Over."

"Seeker, this is Cheyenne, wait for Honcho, Over."

It seemed to take forever for Honcho to get back to them on the radio. The entire team and even the Browns were getting ready to cover one another. The main problem besides the two sniper rifles and the ordinance from the UAV's that were overhead was that they had no support by fire. There would be no Naval Gunfire, Squad weapons to lay down suppressing fire, or even a second element with the strength to overlap with the team. They knew they had a mission, but these were Americans that they were sworn to protect.

"Seeker actual, this is Honcho, be advised, we estimate that the numbers of runners is about fifty, and it looks like they have five or so men on motorcycles baiting them to chase the first element. Eagle says that it is your call, but the fact remains that we need you to make the rendezvous, this mission is for civilization, not just for America. How copy? Over."

Achilles looked at the men, they all wanted to help the people running, no matter if it were a trap, this is what they were trained to do. They were a group of seven with the Browns, they would be outnumbered almost two to one, and they all knew it. They had a few things going for them. Their backs were to a hill, they had the advantage of elevation and the element of surprise. It was now or never, the runners were around 500 meters out, and they would need to start taking them down if they were to have a chance.

"Cheyenne, this is Seeker, we request danger close fire mission from first UAV when the enemy is within 300 meters, we need you to hit them with all you have. We will initiate fire in thirty seconds, be advised, the team is a go for contact, wait out."

Saying 'wait out' is like telling the other person on the end of the line to keep an open end of communication ready, but not to talk until they were spoken to. The team all heard the order and were ready to do their jobs. With that Achilles nodded to Woody and Little Brown, they had the rifles and he told them to take out the men on the motorcycles. The rest of the team would shoot at targets of opportunity as they came into range. Meat and Opie had set up four of their eight claymore mines that the team had between them. They were in a line formation, they had little cover, but that was a good thing. No one should be shooting back, it was just the sheer amount of firepower that they could lay down, and hopefully a large amount of confusion by the runners once the men on the motorcycles went down.

CHAPTER 15
FIGHT OR DIE

The team was all in position, the plan was simple: take out the riders that were corralling the mob of the undead, the people running would be treated as hostiles if they attacked the team. The secondary target was the mob, if the mob turned on them, they would blow the claymores when they got close, and Escape and try to Evade (or E&E) up the side of the mountain that was to their backs.

The little town that was the scene for the set up was probably once a nice place. Mostly desert, but up near the mountains, not much of anything else around. Achilles imagined that it was just one of those places that people never left once they were here.

With fifty of the runners and probably the shamblers somewhere in the three to four hundred range, the team would count on the noise from the motorcycles and explosions that the bombs from the UAV's would make to draw the attention of the undead. The scene was unfolding, Achilles could see the fear in the eyes of the group that was fleeing from the undead masses and the men on the motorcycles. There were few men in the lead group, mostly woman and children. They would be caught once they ran out of gas, or eventually tired of running and finally give up. Who knew how they had made it this far, how they had survived this much of life in this new and uncertain world that was all anyone knew now.

Woody and Little Brown started shooting, two of the motorcycle riders' heads were blown up like watermelon at an old Gallagher concert. They were ones on the farthest wing of the herding process. The rest of the team was shooting at runners. The mass confusion that was unfolding was insane to say the least. "INCOMING!" was screamed over the communication devices from the operator at Cheyenne, and the world rocked as 300 pound laser guided bombs dropped in the middle of the crowd of undead.

Body parts and zombies flew and were burning. The UAV operator announced that all munitions were expended, and Achilles told him to get on the horn with the Chung Hoon and to get those birds in the air. The rest of the team was in free fire mode. Head shots and neck shots were what they were aiming for.

The riders were down to two, one of them was too close to the impact area, and one was off of his bike and running away from the masses. The team watched in horror as he was chased down and runners tore into him. The last rider was gunning it away from the masses. He had no idea what or who was hitting him with this much force.

Achilles called for a cease-fire, they hunkered down and watched things unfold. If they were lucky, the masses would stop and mill about. Maybe the fire from the burning corpses would be enough to cause other shamblers to catch on fire and burn away. They hoped that they could be so lucky. Things in combat generally are so fast, that in the mind's eye they seem to slow down; this is more commonly referred to as the fog of war. Some people think the fog is just on the entire battlefield and something that high up commanders experience, but those on the ground know differently.

The group of people running in the trucks split out like

their hair was on fire. They had no clue who their saviors were, but at this point in time it really didn't matter. They were high tailing it out of the area with no caution. The team silently hoped that they could keep going and make it somewhere safe. The masses of undead were reduced to probably around seventy to a hundred of the undead. These odds were way better for the team. Stewy had told them how he thought that some of the undead seemed to be able to smell the blood of the living; Achilles was hoping that that was untrue.

This was a surreal scene, runners and now shamblers were tearing the men from the motorcycles apart, they were just flesh and bone for the undead, a meal was all that they turned out to be. This may have been good for the team, but there was nowhere near enough food for the undead masses. It was eerily quiet since the last few moments had been filled with explosions and gunfire. Runners seemed to be searching the air for more to eat, they looked almost doglike with a thousand yard stare that some Vietnam veterans were said to have had.

At this point is when the howling began, they sounded like dogs almost with their guttural howls. One of the undead slowly raised its arm as if to point right at the position of the team, and almost as one the entire group of runners and shamblers started to move toward their position. Meat looked at Achilles and nodded, he then told the group to take 'em down, targets of opportunity and not to fall back until Achilles called it out.

Most men in this type of danger would run, there are only people such as soldiers, police officers, and a few select others that would stay and fight against an overwhelming force like this. They all were shooting rapidly in succession. The runners were coming fast, Achilles watched the team take them out, but also knew it in his military mind that they would not be able to drop them all prior to them getting to their position. With that he gave his order. "Little Brown, Moon, Big Brown, Doc, Woody, all of you start climbing now, make for the first ridge and cover us after the claymores go off!" That left Achilles, Meat, and Opie on the ground. Opie and Achilles kept firing for all they were worth.

The first landing was about 20 feet up a rock face that wasn't very difficult to climb. There was a 3-foot ledge that the team was falling back to. Most people would think that this strategy was crazy, but then again there were zombies that were trying to eat the team. So, crazy or not, it was the best option that would give them more time. Meat yelled "COVER!" and Opie and Achilles hit the deck. At that instant the breath was knocked out of each and every person on the team as four daisy chained Claymore mines popped off in succession. A claymore is designed with hundreds of ball bearing and C-4. It can knock down trees and in extreme instances has been used to clear forest for creating an LZ for a helicopter.

The sheer amount of carnage from the blast of the claymore mines was staggering to say the least. Most people take cover behind trees when they are set off, and the entire team was winded and their ears were ringing from the proximity of the blast. The numbers of undead were very low to say the least, there were probably less than twenty-five or so at this point, most of which were shamblers and a few runners, but this enabled the rest of the team to start the climb. Woody was having difficulty making it up the incline, but the rest of the team helped him to get to the ledge.

From this new vantage point the team was making short work of the rest of the undead in the area. Head shots and the conservation of ammunition was the most important thing for the time being. The mines had helped to give them a dire break in the swell of undead, but at this point who knew how many more would start to converge due to the sound of the blast.

"Cheyenne, this is Seeker 06, can we get a wide range scan before the UAV's head back to rearm and refuel? Over. Also need a sitrep from the birds that are supposed to be en-route at this time, Over."

"Seeker, this is Cheyenne, we are getting that Sitrep at this time, be advised, we are sweeping the area for any more of the tangos in the area, Over."

The team took a few moments to reload their weapons, drink water to stay hydrated, and also to deal with the shock that they all felt from the blast of four highly concussive explosions in such a close proximity. The only person to truly look to be reeling from the blast was the Doc, and he really just could only say "Wow!" He was amazed at the amount of carnage that the team had dealt in such a short period of time. The fact that it was only undead, and no one had shot a single shot back at them was probably why he was handling it so well.

"Seeker, this is Cheyenne, we estimate pickup now to be just after dark, the pickup team requests use of green chem.-lights to mark where you will be, also to turn on your ELT's when they are 30 minutes out. Recon shows a few pockets of undead to be heading in your direction, they don't seem to be moving very fast, most of what we can tell that are coming your way are shamblers. Honcho suggests to try to make for a building near the LZ where you can access the roof for pickup, how copy? Over."

"Good copy Cheyenne, we will mop up and get a move on to a good location, ELT's will be on as soon as we are 30 mics out from pickup. Out."

Achilles told the rest of the team about the ELT's (Electronic Location transmitters), had everyone cross-load and redistribute ammunition, and laid out the plan for the team. It was time to have a talk with the Browns about them coming on board or getting out of Dodge. This was a conversation that he knew he needed to have, and they probably were expecting it anyway. He decided that once they were in a secure position he would lay it out for them.

Everyone scaled back down the ridge, it had been a lucky position to take up. If they would not have had an egress route they probably could have lost a member or two to the hoard. They loaded up in one of the trucks and made for the town.

It took the team roughly all of an half hour to get down and make it to what looked to be the sturdiest building with the biggest roof. It was on the main drag, or basically the only paved road that was running through the area. The plan was simple, two members of the team would go in, clear the structure and find the roof access, then they would go up top, eat, and defend the position as necessary while they waited for their ride.

Opie and Meat took the job of securing the inside of the building. Both were going in with 12 gauge shotguns for close quarters combat if needed, and the rest of the team would secure the main door. After it was clear, the Browns' truck would be moved to blockade the entrance to the old auto parts store that they were using as a new base of operations for the time being.

The two member shooter team went inside and went to work clearing the building. It was eerily silent, and they had to check the corners and aisles of the store. All they found was the remains of what looked to be two people that had been eaten alive. There was no way with the amount of damage that they had taken from the undead that they would ever be able to reanimate. They found the ladder to the roof, cleared it, and informed the rest of the team that it was clear. This was as good a time as any for Achilles to have that conversation with the Browns.

Everyone made their way up to the roof. They pulled the ladder up to keep anyone or anything from climbing up top with them, and also had set up on all four corners to keep an eye out for anything coming toward them. As long as the pickup happened in the next few hours they were as safe as they could be in this backend little town.

Achilles started with saying to the Browns, "Guys, I know that you are making your way west and trying to find out anything that you can about your family. I understand and it is very honorable for you to do this. I know that I swore you in, and when we are gone you have full authority to do what you can as members of this new version of the government and the Army. We appreciate everything that you have done for us, and can leave you a way to communicate with Cheyenne, and even a few things that we have to help you in your endeavor. However, I would like for you both to consider coming along with us on our journey. We are going to try to find a cure, vaccine, or something to help us keep mankind alive long enough to reclaim our nation, and sometime down the road hopefully the planet. I know that this decision won't be easy, and I don't want you to rush into it, but the offer is there for you to help us out. We'll be picked up in a few hours, so why don't you think it over."

Both of the Browns looked relieved and shocked almost at once. They had obviously spoken to each other about what would happen when they parted ways with the team. If they went their own way they knew that it was only a matter of time before they ran into a swarm, or a large swarm found them that they would not be able to outrun. Father and son had done more than many members of the military's special operations community had been able to do. The look they consisted of a few nods, then Big Brown spoke after a short silence.

"Sir, we would be happy to come along. We know what our fate is if it is just the two of us, and we know that it is no more than a pipe dream that we have any members of our family left. We have been lying to ourselves. To be honest, we know that we have been really lucky to have made it this far on our own, and between the bandits, rogue military forces, and undead we really consider ourselves fortunate to be alive. So if you think that we can help, we would like to continue on your journey with you. Our training is good, and we know how to deal with the undead, so that is our decision."

In the distance the team heard the sound of an aircraft, a

look of satisfaction fell upon their faces, and they new that this was just the beginning of what they were going to experience as a team. Achilles knew that the next few weeks and months would be long, treacherous, and possibly deadly. He knew it and was ready to try and make a difference, a difference for himself, and for all of humanity...

Coming Soon

The Mission: Patient Zero

{ A Military and Zombie Apocalypse Series }

3 Years After... Book 2

ABOUT THE AUTHOR

G.R. Mountjoy is a first time author who recently became very interested in Zombie/Apocalypse books. *3 Years After...* is his first novel.

Mr. Mountjoy is a medically retired Soldier from the United States Army. He enjoys golf, sports, television, and being around the water. He lives with his gorgeous wife, and beautiful daughter.